A CRITERION BOOK
FOR YOUNG PEOPLE

THE GOLDEN IMPALA

THE

GOLDEN

MPALA

By Pamela Ropner

Illustrated by Ralph Thompson

CRITERION BOOKS • NEW YORK

CONTENTS

one	A STRANGE VISITOR	11
two	OLD JABULA	17
three	THE TREK	23
four	UMSINSI REST CAMP	31
five	PETER'S MUSEUM	39
six	DISTURBING NEWS	49
seven	MERIBI DRIFT	55
eight	BLUE WILDEBEEST FARM	67
nine	THE LEGEND	77
ten	MISSING	81
eleven	PETER ALONE	91
twelve	THE CAVE	97
thirteen	UMOSOGO	107
fourteen	LOST	117

fifteen   LEROUX   127

sixteen   THE FOURTH TIME   137

seventeen   SIGN IN THE DUST   145

eighteen   THE MARK   151

                 GLOSSARY   157

THE GOLDEN IMPALA

A STRANGE VISITOR

THE impala is the loveliest of all African antelope. There is nothing in the world more beautiful than a herd of impala in full flight." Peter's father spoke slowly and with conviction. "It is something that, once seen, you can never forget."

Peter hoped this was the beginning of one of his father's wonderful animal stories. But Mr. Ward was silent. He puffed gently at his pipe and stared thoughtfully into the fire.

"Peter!" Mrs. Ward's voice sounded from the room above. "Peter!" She sounded impatient. Reluctantly Peter got up. He did not feel at all like going to bed now.

Mr. Ward smiled at his son sympathetically. "Off you go!" he said. "Tell you what, tomorrow or the next day I'll take you on a trek."

Peter's face brightened. He waited a moment. Then,

11

as his father said nothing more, he slowly left the room.

Ten years ago Hector Ward had been an experienced hunter. Then he had become warden of the Taluki Game Reserve, exchanging his gun for a camera. As warden, he helped protect the animals that he had once hunted. He and his wife and Peter, their twelve-year-old son, lived in Thabankwe House, on the Reserve.

Mrs. Ward was not altogether happy there. She had always been frightened of the bush, with its daytime noises and nameless rustlings, and its startling sudden cries at night. But Peter loved Thabankwe House, the Taluki Reserve, and the bush. That he had no companions of his own age did not worry him. The creatures that lived in the bush were all he sought for company. When he was away at school, he waited only for the day when he would return to the Reserve, and he looked forward to the time when he could spend his life uninterrupted in the African grassland—the bushveldt.*

Slowly Peter climbed the polished hardwood stairs. Halfway up he stopped to admire the photographs of game animals that hung in long rows on the paneled wall of the landing. As he looked at the one of two crocodiles lying in unsuspecting ease on the banks of the Zambesi, he remembered the first time he had seen a crocodile. It had turned its hostile gaze on him, and he had looked into green, glassy eyes as cold and cruel as icy seas. Peter smiled at the photograph of the swift, dappled cheetah playing with her cubs, and at the mag-

---

* For special words used in South Africa but unfamiliar to us, consult the glossary at the end of this book.

nificent shot of a charging elephant. The huge ears were outstretched and the trunk raised menacingly. This was one of his father's most remarkable photographs. He passed it slowly and went into his room.

Peter's small bedroom looked over the garden to the line of gum trees that marked the end of the garden and the beginning of the bush. On the walls hung gaily patterned gourds, numerous snakeskins, African war drums, and a sharply pointed wooden spear tipped with iron—the assagai. Weird masks grinned from the corners. On the bedside table lay a necklace of lions' claws, brown with age; Peter had been given this by an old Swazi, who swore that it had no equal as a lucky charm to ward off all devils.

Peter stood for a moment looking at his possessions with satisfaction. He knew that his mother never entered his room without a shudder, and he appreciated her leaving his treasures alone even when he was away at school. She had long since learned how useless it was to try to curb a collector's enthusiasm. Her husband's trophies, skins, and photographs occupied nearly every inch of wall space in the small house.

Usually Peter did not hurry to bed, but tonight he was tired. He undressed quickly, touched the lions'-claw necklace (although he pretended not to believe in such superstitions) and slipped between the sheets.

Peter was already fast asleep when his father and mother came to say goodnight to him. They looked lovingly at the tall, slightly built boy, whose almost delicate appearance hid a steely strength and extraordinary stamina. Then they went to their room. Soon all was quiet in Thabankwe House.

In the night Peter awoke, he did not know why. Outside, the moon shone palely through the swaying trees. The house was silent. He listened intently, then from the garden there came a curious but distinct rustling, as of something running lightly through the bushes.

Peter got out of bed. Quietly he tiptoed to the window, the monkey rug warm beneath his feet. Someone had left a light burning in the room below, and the window was reflected on the lawn. At first Peter could see nothing in the garden, for a sudden dark cloud hid the moon. He stared out into the night until his eyes became accustomed to the thick blackness. What he saw then made him catch his breath.

The whole garden was alive with moving creatures! One of the dark shapes detached itself from the shadows and leaped lightly over the grass. The swift, lithe form was caught momentarily in the square of light from the window. Excitedly Peter saw that it was an impala. A second impala came into the light for a brief moment. Another followed, then another and another, until Peter lost count of the graceful, swerving forms. Abruptly all movement ceased, as suddenly as it had begun; and the garden seemed deserted. Peter shivered a little, and turned away from the window. Then some instinct made him glance back.

There, in the yellow pool of light, stood a lone impala. It was poised on legs as fine and slender as spun

glass. The tiny, delicate hoofs seemed scarcely to imprint the ground. The little animal raised its head and for a second Peter looked down into its huge, sad eyes. Then, with a nervous flicking of its ears, the impala sprang a few paces beyond the square of light.

Peter gripped the window sill breathlessly, for in the darkness the impala shone with a soft golden light. Again it turned its head, and the slender arched horns gleamed and sparkled.

As Peter leaned forward to look at the magical creature, his foot struck an old war drum with a shattering clatter. Peter glanced down at the drum. When he looked out again, the garden was empty. The cloud had passed from before the moon, and once more the scene was flooded in its pale light.

For a long time Peter waited, but nothing more came out of the night. Reluctantly he returned to bed, but it was a long time before he went to sleep.

OLD JABULA

*P*ETER awoke late the next morning. The events of the night almost forgotten, he lay for a moment, enjoying the delicious smell of breakfast that floated up from the kitchen. Then hastily he washed, pulled on his khaki shorts and shirt, and ran cheerfully down the stairs to the breakfast room. Hungrily he tackled the large plate of brown porridge, the fried sweet potatoes, and bacon.

Through the long windows that opened out on the covered porch or stoop, Peter could see his father staring at the garden. A moment later he came into the room, frowning slightly.

"What is it, Father?" asked Peter. But as he spoke, he quite suddenly knew what was the matter.

Mr. Ward spoke slowly. "The garden and the bush for a great distance around are covered with impala spoor. Your mother's precious roses are all trampled and broken. There must have been thousands of the creatures. We'll have to make the fence higher."

Still frowning, he went into his study.

Peter left his breakfast unfinished. He ran out of the long window onto the stoop, and from there into the garden.

It was a dazzling morning; the garden had never looked more beautiful. The red and white poinsettias were like colored stars against the deep blue sky. Privately Peter preferred these flamboyant flowers to the roses that were his mother's pride and joy, reminding her of her home in England. These roses were now crushed and trampled into the red soil, which was imprinted with sharp little hoofs. Beside one of the flower beds lay his mother's trowel. Evidently she had already been out, vainly trying to repair the damage. He wondered where she was now.

Peter walked on, to the small green patch of lawn that lay between the house and the garden. For the sake of that small green patch, Mr. Ward waged an unceasing battle against the burning sun. Water sprinklers whirled and hummed there all day long. A cheerful native—a Basuto—was responsible for seeing that the stream of water never ceased.

Peter crossed the lawn and stood beneath the living-room window. A solitary sun bird fluttered through the air above him, the sun glinting on its gleaming metallic plumage. Somewhere in the trees a hoopoe shrilled. No one was in sight.

With his eye Peter measured the distance to his bedroom window above, then knelt down and looked searchingly at the place where he judged the Golden Impala to have stood. As he ran his fingers over the short blades of grass, a slight movement behind him made him glance over his shoulder. Jabula, the gardener, stood looking down at him.

Jabula was a very old man, exactly how old no one knew. One morning, many years before, Mr. Ward had gone out and found Jabula sitting on the stoop. The old man had asked for a week's work in the garden. The week had extended into a month, and the month into years.

There was no man alive who knew more than Jabula about the secrets of the bushveldt. He had a never-failing supply of fascinating stories which he would recount in halting English. And he could give wonderfully real imitations of the calls and sounds of the bush birds and animals.

Peter looked up into a pair of sharp, black eyes set deep in the wrinkled face.

"*Sakubona,* Jabula."

"*Sakubona, Nkosana,*" replied the old man, unsmiling. "What are you looking for?"

Peter hesitated; then he said, "I am looking for spoor. There must have been thousands of impala in the garden last night."

"There are often impala in the garden," said Old Jabula.

"But there were *thousands* of them, I saw them myself from my window."

A curious expression flickered briefly over the old man's face, but he did not speak.

"I saw them," Peter continued, "and there was one different from the rest. It shone, Jabula! It shone like gold!"

Jabula did not answer, but Peter's keen eyes noticed the swift tensing of his body.

"You know something, Jabula," Peter said. "Tell me what it is. Tell me about the Golden Impala."

In his eagerness the boy's voice rose. He looked as if he were trying to read the answer to the mystery in the wise black face. But there was no reply to the boy's insistent questions. Instead, the old man half turned to go.

As he moved, one of the lion's claws that he wore around his neck fell to the ground. Jabula bent low to pick it up. His thin fingers closed on the claw. Still stooping, he spoke so softly that Peter could barely catch the words. "The time is not yet, *Nkosana*."

The next instant Jabula straightened up, turned, and shuffled off into the green shadows of the garden.

"Good morning, darling." Peter's mother was calling from the stoop, where she was arranging the remnants of the roses in a large blue bowl.

"You were having a very absorbing conversation with Old Jabula," she said as Peter walked over toward her. "What were you discussing so intently?"

"Nothing much, Mother," Peter replied. He wondered if he should tell her what had happened, but something held him back. He stooped to pick up one of the broken roses; the thorn pricked him and he dropped it.

"Peter, dear, go and get me my flower catalogues, please. They're in the gun room."

Glad of an excuse to leave, Peter went into the house.

The gun room smelled pleasantly of oil and leather. Idly Peter glanced up at a stuffed impala head. The fixed glass eyes regarded him coldly. He looked away and turned to search for the catalogues. He found them easily and carried them to his mother, glad to be out again in the warm, bright sunlight.

THE TREK

THE insistent shrill of the alarm woke Peter. He glanced at the luminous clock dial—four o'clock. He lay still for a moment, wondering sleepily why he was being waked up at this early hour. Then suddenly he remembered that today he was going on a trek through the bush with his father. They were going to a water hole where lion had been seen only a few days before, and they must start early in order to reach the watering place before dawn. There they would lie in hiding and watch as the animals came down to drink after their night of hunting and being hunted.

Peter's father tiptoed into the room. "Hurry up, Peter," he whispered. "If we are lucky we might see a kill. Then we'll go on to Richard Hutchison's at Umsinsi Rest Camp. Be quiet, so you won't wake your mother. There's tea downstairs when you're ready."

Mr. Ward had been on so many treks that he had long since lost count of them. Yet each time he was stirred by the same excitement that had always gripped him when, as a boy, he had gone with his father. He wondered if his son felt the same way.

Peter pulled on his thick green sweater and heavy boots, and unhooked his binoculars from above his bed. Then he went down through the dark hall into the breakfast room.

The tea was scalding hot. Peter felt its comforting glow as he drank as quickly as he could. He knew that his father was impatient to be off.

"Time to go," said Mr. Ward. "We'll have to hurry if we're to reach the river before dawn." He shouldered his old, well-used rifle and handed another to his son, with the warning: "Don't use it unless I tell you."

Outside, a tall native waited.

"Ready, Umosogo?" said Mr. Ward. Umosogo grinned, his teeth showing very white.

Mr. Ward led the way, Peter followed, and Umosogo brought up the rear, his bare feet moving noiselessly over the ground. They passed through the garden and plunged into the bush. Mr. Ward switched on his flashlight.

"We'll go this way," he said. He turned and set off along a narrow track. He walked briskly, though alert for any possible danger.

Peter did not find the going easy. It was still dark, and he could not see to avoid the vicious, whippy branches that hung over the path. Often they struck him sharply on the face. He tried to ignore their painful sting, and plunged resolutely after the wavering beam of the torch. Ahead the fireflies flickered like wandering sparks.

Without speaking, the three tramped on through the bush. A slight wind stirred the branches of the trees. Sometimes a tiny muskrat was caught in the beam of light. Once a guinea fowl, rudely disturbed, clattered noisily away, shrilling an alarm to its fellows in the undergrowth. Far off a jackal howled. Peter listened intently for the roar of a lion. He knew well that the jackal, tireless scavenger of the bush, would follow the lion, hoping for some remnant of its kill. But only the husky cough of a baboon broke the silence.

Peter judged that they had been walking for over an hour when his father slowed his easy, regular stride and waited. Peter drew abreast of him. Mr. Ward switched off the flashlight.

"We are near the river now. Keep very quiet, and we'll find a hideout."

The trees were thinning now, and the low murmur of the water sounded in their ears. On either side of the path grew fantastically tall elephant grass. It was well named, for an elephant could lurk in it undetected. Peter could not help wondering what dangerous beast might lie there unseen. Hastily he dismissed this uncomfortable thought from his mind, but his fingers tightened around the butt of his rifle.

Mr. Ward stopped. The river broadened at this point, and the banks sloped easily to the water's edge. He motioned to Peter and Umosogo to crouch down. "Mustn't show ourselves on the skyline," he murmured in Peter's ear.

The small party crept through the grass until they were near the river bank. To their right grew a low, thick line of thorn bushes. Mr. Ward signaled with his hand that they were to kneel behind these. When dawn came they would have a clear view of the river, through the twining branches, but would be hidden from watching eyes.

"It's more usual for the antelopes to drink at noon, but they have often been seen here at dawn. Good watering place. Quite shallow." Mr. Ward spoke very low.

Peter took the generous lump of biltong his father gave him. He loved the sharp spicy flavor of the sun-dried meat. As he chewed it he tried to feel like an experienced hunter.

A delicate rose lightened the horizon over which a few slim, dark pencils of cloud hovered. As Peter watched, the clouds slowly turned from black to a rich purple, then to the palest violet. The burning rim of the sun slid slowly over the horizon with its black, silhouetted trees, and another day dawned over Africa. The darkness melted into light. Frightening huddled shapes revealed themselves as nothing more fearful than scrub and thorn bushes, and the nameless terrors of the night retreated before the brightness of the day.

Downstream a hippo blew the water noisily from its large nostrils, and grunted contentedly as it shook the drops from its round ears. A white-headed sea eagle screamed cheerfully overhead; its high, musical call, heard on every African river, drifted down to the watchers on the morning wind.

Peter felt a nudge and followed his father's gaze. Two water buck were picking their way down the river banks. They moved slowly, stopping to sniff the air suspiciously. Then, satisfied that all was well, they lowered their heads to drink.

A small herd of blue wildebeest approached in cautious single file. Some twenty yards short of the water, as if by some unspoken word of command, they whirled around and charged back the way they had come. Their heads were down, their tails waving wildly. Peter recognized this strange behavior as a trick to draw out any enemy that might be lurking near the water's edge. The wildebeest halted, and Peter held his breath. Nothing stirred, so once more the wildebeest returned to the river, grunting and calling noisily to each other. Peter thought them curious looking—half cow, half horse— their heavy bearded heads contrasting oddly with their elegantly sloping hindquarters and swinging tufted tails. Other wildebeest, made bold by their fellows, trotted down to drink. One lean old bull, his purplish hide much scarred, did sentry duty on the bank above them. He stood absolutely motionless, like a carved wooden figure, every nerve and sinew alert for any sound of danger.

Several zebra, inseparable companion of the wildebeest, bustled down to the water's edge in a whirl of stripes, tossing tails, and twitching flanks. They kicked up their polished heels and whinnied constantly to each other.

A tiny steen buck passed so close to Peter that he could see its huge, long-lashed eyes and the delicate prick of its sensitive ears. The buck drank in long, nervous gulps, poised for instant flight. A small carelessness, a relaxing of ceaseless vigilance, could mean death. Poor little buck, thought Peter, you have so many enemies! He wondered what terrors the night had held for the gentle little creature.

Three kudoo emerged from the shadows. The old bull was a magnificent specimen. His great looped and spiraled horns were the largest that Peter had ever seen. The kudoo drank eagerly. They did not even raise their heads when a number of impala glided into view on the opposite bank and came down to drink. They stood silhouetted against the light; then, as if by some secret signal that all was well, impala began to appear on all sides—twenty, fifty, two hundred. Soon Peter lost all count of them.

Beside him, Mr. Ward reached for his binoculars. Peter saw that his father was frowning. The opposite river bank had become a swaying mass of chestnut bodies and graceful curving horns. A large part of the herd waded through the shallow water to the other side. Still they came—thousands of them. Umosogo shifted uneasily. Hector Ward murmured, "I cannot understand it. I've never seen so many. Where have they all come from? And all so thirsty at this time of day."

No one answered. Fascinated, they watched as wave

after wave of impala surged through the water and up the bank. They trod so lightly that they seemed scarcely to touch the ground.

Then, in the distance, a lion roared. The air seemed to vibrate with the sound. In an instant the impala were thrown into confusion. They paused for a timeless moment before terror struck, then fled for the protection of the bush. They did not know in what direction safety lay; they only knew that they must flee headlong or perish. Hundreds of the terrified animals, heads thrown back, slender horns tilted against their necks, flashed by so close to Peter that he could see the black fringe of hair on their slim fetlocks.

Then they were gone. A solitary hoopoe called. A monkey chattered hysterically. Slowly the yellow mud settled back on the river bed.

Mr. Ward stood up. "We'll not see a lion now, Peter, so we had better be going." For another moment they waited, then left the river bank and went on their way.

UMSINSI REST CAMP

ICHARD Hutchison, warden of the Umsinsi Rest Camp on the Taluki Game Reserve, stood at the door of his hut and looked out at the new day. He was not a tall man, but strongly built, with huge hands, and muscles standing out like cords in his powerful arms.

He narrowed his clear eyes against the strong light. Yawning a little, he pushed a most unusual hat farther back on his black hair. This hat was the subject of much discussion among the native boys. It was said to have magic properties of considerable power. Had not *Inkosi* emerged unscathed from some exceedingly dangerous situations? And every time he had been wearing the hat!

Actually, Richard Hutchison owed his life to his own matchless skill with a gun and his solid British calm in the face of danger. The hat was only a battered Stetson that some friend had brought him from America. But, knowing the value of superstition, he did not deny the possibility that it possessed more than ordinary powers.

As warden of the Rest Camp, he was responsible for enforcing the few but necessary rules. He knew every inch of the Reserve, and loved and understood the animals that roamed there. He liked the heat, the rains, the dust, the cruelty and the beauty of it all, and would not have exchanged his lonely warden's house for all the marble palaces in the world.

It had been a particularly lovely dawn, Richard Hutchison reflected as, glancing toward the gate, he saw Peter and his father enter, followed by Umosogo. Grinning widely, he strode toward them. He took Peter's small hand in his huge one and slapped Hector Ward's back so vigorously that he winced.

"Who's ready for breakfast?" he boomed cheerfully.

"Me!" shouted Peter with such enthusiasm that the others laughed.

"Come on then," said Hutchison. They followed him into the pleasant shade of the house. On the long wooden table in the dining room breakfast was laid out —*maltabella,* the dark, chocolate-colored mealie porridge; golden corn cobs in butter; melons; great orange slices of paw-paw; and a large platter of bacon, eggs, and chops.

Peter ate until he could eat no more. He pushed back his plate and looked with interest around the room.

The walls held shelves which were loaded with countless carvings of animals, for Richard Hutchison was a carver of no mean skill. Years ago a native guide had taught him the art and it continued to fascinate him. He was often to be seen whittling away at a piece of hardwood: Peter loved to watch an elephant or fat hippo take shape beneath his skillful fingers.

On the walls hung game trophies and a network of horns. Peter gazed with awe at the magnificent head of a sable antelope with its long, deadly, needle-sharp horns. He knew that a cornered, desperate sable is a very dangerous opponent; the slash and sweep of its horns can cut an enemy to ribbons.

On each side of the hearth stood a gigantic tusk, beautifully mounted in silver.

Richard Hutchison's eyes followed Peter's fascinated gaze. "That brute nearly cost me my life."

"Tell me about it," cried Peter enthusiastically.

"I was hunting for ivory in those days," Richard began. "It was dangerous work. An elephant hunter's life lasts no more than four years on the average. I had been hunting for about seven, not without some narrow escapes. Still, I was beginning to feel confident that I was a match for the elephant. That's the time to watch out, as anyone who has lived through it will tell you."

He smiled again, but more grimly now.

"I was tracking a large herd through the bush. There were several fine bulls and a number of cows with their calves. I knew they were near, for the tracks were very fresh. Suddenly I heard a branch crack. Gazing through the bush, I saw the leaves of a wild plum tree swaying wildly. Another crack and the tree toppled, and a really splendid bull elephant emerged. His tusks were exactly what I needed to make up a load which I was due to send down the coast.

"I glanced around me, but could see no other movement. The tusker moved behind a tree. Seizing my chance, I slipped through the bush until I was a mere twenty yards from the huge beast. The elephant was still feasting on the plum tree. It had been growing on the banks of a small water hole, green, stinking, and horrible. I raised my gun. As I did so, I heard a shrill scream of rage behind me. I spun around. There, at the edge of the thicket, I saw to my horror a cow elephant. I knew that she had warned the herd and that my retreat was cut off. I was sure of what must happen.

"I turned as the bull elephant—my intended easy victim—put down his trunk and charged. I still remember the hairy tip of his trunk stretched out to seize my neck as I fired. The elephant staggered and fell.

"I had my prize, but I knew for certain that I was surrounded by the herd. To get away was impossible; to remain was certain death. I felt then the terror that must have come to so many elephant hunters in their last hours. With hardly a thought, I rushed headlong toward the green stinking pool. I plunged in, heedless of the danger of crocodiles, leeches, or disease. With only my nose above the water, I lay there for hours, while the great beasts tramped and pushed around the body of their dead companion. Then, as silently as only elephants can move, they wandered off through the forest. When daylight faded I climbed out of the nasty pool and spent the rest of that night in a tree.

"I never sold the great tusks but kept them by me as a reminder of the lesson they taught me—that it never does to think oneself a match for an elephant. Never forget that, young Pete."

"I won't," promised Peter. Then, to prolong the conversation, he asked, "What makes an elephant a rogue?"

"Toothache," Richard answered surprisingly. "That was an old beast and one of his tusks was very loose. Probably it gave the poor creature a great deal of pain."

He fell silent and lit a cigarette. Then he said briskly, "Off you go, son, I've something to discuss with your father."

Always the same, thought Peter. Whenever there is something interesting going on, I'm politely told to go away. He said nothing, but he took as long as possible to leave the room.

Outside it was very hot. The native boys sat around idle, and the yellow Kaffir dogs snarled and growled their discontent.

Umosogo leaned carelessly against a tree. Peter looked at his tall, wiry figure admiringly. Umosogo was no ordinary Zulu. He was the son of a chief and had inherited his father's proud bearing and arrogant tilt of the head. None of the other boys dared take any liberties with Umosogo. He was renowned for his great strength and cunning. Who else could throw a spear with such deadly accuracy or run through the bush with such speed? Mr. Ward often said that he would have to search all Africa to find a more loyal and valuable servant.

Peter wandered past the neat *rondavels,* little one-roomed round houses that provided shelter for the night for the visitors to the camp. Each stood tidily in its own patch of ground, white walls gleaming, the conical thatched roofs black in the strong sunlight. Peter glanced through an open, green-painted door; inside a man lay asleep, carelessly huddled on the iron bed. The boy passed quietly on toward the fence that marked the boundary of the camp.

Two men leaned against it, deep in conversation. They did not look around as Peter walked toward them. When he was some fifty yards away, he stopped and stood watching them. One was short and dark and in no way remarkable. The other was very different—immensely tall and powerfully built, with a shock of copper hair.

Peter was filled with an unreasonable desire to hear what the two men were saying. The small man talked rapidly, often pointing in the direction of the bush. The other nodded repeatedly but spoke little.

Peter approached until he was within a few yards of them. Not for nothing had he learned the art of silent tracking from Umosogo! He stopped, scarcely breathing, and listened intently. He heard but one word— *impala.* He began to creep closer, but in his eagerness he forgot his caution, and his foot struck a stone.

The two men whirled around to face the boy. As the tall one leaned forward, Peter looked into blue eyes as cold as ice and holding more than a hint of menace. The lower half of the man's face, Peter noticed, was covered by a magnificent, curling, red beard.

The small man spoke angrily. "So you spy on us, boy!" His thin voice rose. "Do you know what happens to spies?" Peter was too unnerved to answer.

The small man added nastily, "Take care, boy. Some very unpleasant things can happen to spies."

The tall man broke in suddenly, in a deep, growling voice. "Do not be alarmed, boy. My friend here is only joking." He indicated his companion with a half-contemptuous gesture. "We were discussing the habits of game. Not a very mysterious conversation, I fear." He smiled at Peter, but there was no warmth in the smile.

Peter knew, with a strange certainty, that the tall man was lying, but he merely smiled back and nodded.

Then the tall man looked away from Peter. Staring into the distance, he fingered his thick beard. "So you play the hunter?" he said, as if to himself. "Take care that the hunter doesn't become the hunted." The words held an unmistakable note of warning.

Abruptly the tall man turned on his heel and, motioning the other to follow, strode away.

Peter watched them until they had disappeared behind the *rondavels*. Questions raced through his mind. What were the two men discussing that they did not wish to be overheard? Was it merely coincidence that he had heard the word "impala"? What was it that the tall man had said about the hunter and the hunted? He gazed into the bush, almost as if he expected to read there the answers to his questions.

On the dry, cracked earth lay a green lizard, basking idly in the brilliant sun. It regarded Peter with gleaming, jeweled eyes, but at his first movement it scuttled away.

Peter saw his father coming toward him. Richard Hutchison was a few paces behind.

"Oh, there you are, Peter," Mr. Ward said. "We've been looking for you. Richard is going to drive us back home."

As they strolled toward the car, Peter said, "Father, did you see two men as you came through the camp? One was short and dark; the other was very tall, with a great red beard?"

Mr. Ward shook his head.

"I've seen them around," Richard Hutchison said. "They've been staying at the Rest Camp. Why do you ask? Have you been talking to them?"

"No," answered Peter. "I just saw them."

And he wondered to himself why he had answered this way.

FIVE

PETER'S MUSEUM

THE next few days passed uneventfully. Peter's father and mother were very busy, so Peter was often left to himself. One day, when it was too hot to do anything that required much energy, he decided to examine and catalogue his museum.

He went up to his bedroom, turned on the fan, and stood for a moment enjoying the cooling breeze. Then he pulled out from under the bed a large mahogany box. This was his museum.

It did not contain anything that was startlingly rare or of great antiquity, but Peter knew and loved every one of the dusty exhibits. He liked to finger them gently, remembering where and when they had come into his possession. He had always meant to catalogue them but somehow had never got around to it.

He looked down with pride at his collection. He picked up the ostrich egg and ran his finger over its smooth, creamy surface. Putting it down, he bent to examine the beautifully ornamented blowpipe a friend of his father's had sent him from the Congo. Inside lay some tiny darts. They were not poison ones; still, he handled the object with care.

One by one he lifted out his treasures. Locusts, cast-off snakeskins, a carved wooden Zulu pillow, beadwork of all kinds, small idols that Umosogo had given him; even a large empty tortoise shell. Many of these things, he had been told, had impressive magic properties. Umosogo had explained some of them to him in great detail. Peter had lived too long in the bush to disbelieve these stories entirely. So far the charms had not had any undue influence on his life, but one never knew.

He plucked at the string of his *ugubu,* a musical instrument shaped like a bow. It gave a melodious, twanging sound. He dusted his wooden animals, a beautiful little clay model of a giraffe, and his *lesiba*—a pipe often used by Basuto herd boys. At the bottom of the box was a Swazi snuffbox and two hollowed gourds gorgeously patterned in red and ochre. Peter lifted them out, blew inside, and laid them down again. The box now empty, he picked up the sheet of newspaper lining the bottom of it. The paper was dusty and stained. As he shook the dust from the faded print, he scanned it idly. A short paragraph headed "Interesting Zoological Experiments" caught his eye. He began to read. Gradually his interest quickened and he leaned eagerly forward, intent on the printed words:

In order to conduct a series of experiments, the eminent zoologist Professor Hardy has arrived in Johannesburg from London. It is understood that he is exploring the possible scientific value of rare glandular secretions to be found only in certain African animals.

Peter read the paragraph again, frowning. He glanced at the date of the paper; it was six months old. The museum momentarily forgotten, he rose and crossed to the window to read the item for the third time.

Below, the continuous murmur of voices rose and fell as Hector Ward and Richard Hutchison paced up and down on the lawn, talking.

Peter folded the sheet of paper and laid it on the table by his bed. Picking up a red crayon, he marked the paragraph with a faint cross. For a moment he stood looking down at it. Then, half-heartedly, he knelt down to return the objects to the box and push it back under the bed. He noticed the African drum which lay where it had rolled two nights ago. He picked it up and drummed his fingers nervously on the stretched skin. Even in the sunlit peace of the bedroom, the drum vibrated ominously.

Peter began to think of all the strange things he had seen. Did the experiments of that scientist have anything to do with the impala? Why did he somehow feel that they did? He was convinced that the appearance of the Golden Impala was no dream. But what had Old Jabula meant when he said, "The time is not yet"? The time for what?

He must go to Jabula and ask him the meaning of his words. He would go tonight when the old man had finished his work and was cooking his supper over the fire.

The rest of the day passed slowly. Peter tried to amuse himself with one thing and then another, but somehow nothing seemed to interest him. His father and Richard Hutchison were still busy with their discussion, and Mrs. Ward was deep in her flower catalogues.

Evening came. Purple shadows dappled the grass, the sunset clouds glowed and flickered, then faded as the darkness spread over the sky. In the brief half-light, fruit bats swooped and whirled, and the fireflies glimmered softly.

As soon as night fell over the bushveldt, Peter slipped through the house and out the back door. He crossed the yard and followed the path that led to the kraal where Old Jabula lived. This enclosure was some distance from the house. Peter walked steadily along the well-beaten track.

As he approached he could see the flicker of flames. Old Jabula sat huddled over the glowing embers on which a large black pot of porridge was bubbling. In the uncertain light of the fire he looked older and wiser than ever. He did not look up as Peter came near. Peter crouched down and waited, for he knew that it was useless to question the old man until he was ready to speak. The fire crackled and the smoke spiraled in the darkness.

"Why does the young master seek Jabula?" The old man spoke suddenly, but still he did not look at his visitor.

"I have come," said Peter, "to talk to you who are old and wise. Only you can answer my questions." With a slight movement of his head Jabula indicated that he was listening.

Peter spoke again. "Tell me why all at once there are many, many impala in the Reserve. Tell me the meaning of the one which is not like the rest."

The old man sat as if turned to stone. He scarcely seemed to breathe.

"Tell me the meaning of the Golden Impala," Peter begged again.

The fire spluttered; a few sparks glittered briefly. Peter waited, scarcely able to contain his eagerness. It seemed an eternity before the old man replied.

"Why does the *Nkosana* seek to know of *Okhanyayo,* the Shining One?"

"Because," said Peter with emphasis, "I have seen the Golden Impala from my window, and you know I have."

Abruptly, the old man raised his eyes to the boy's face. For a long moment they faced each other over the fire.

"So you have seen the Shining One. The time will come soon—the time is not yet." He fell silent.

Peter half shouted in his eagerness. "What do you

mean, Jabula? Tell me the meaning of your words, for I do not understand."

Jabula answered in a curious chanting voice, as though he were repeating something learned by heart. He spoke slowly and with many pauses, as if the words were buried deep in his memory.

"Four times shall you see the Shining One," Jabula chanted. "Once, twice, thrice—" the old man nodded— "but beware the fourth time, *Nkosana*. Beware the fourth time." The voice trailed off into a croaking whisper, then ceased.

Peter waited, but the old man stood up, folded the red mottled blanket around him, and strode into his hut.

For a time Peter did not move, not wanting to leave the comforting glow of the fire. Beyond the red circle of light the night seemed very black. At last he rose and began to retrace his steps along the path that led to the house.

On either side of the narrow track grew tall trees, and the underbush was thick. Peter realized he was a fool to have come out alone, armed only with his knife.

As he walked it seemed to him that the night was alive with tiny rustling sounds. Once he caught the luminous gleam of eyes peering through the leaves. He walked on resolutely, trying not to hurry.

Then, directly behind him, something stirred in the bushes. Peter halted. He could feel the quick pounding of his heart. He listened intently. Again he walked forward. Again he heard a noise, this time slightly ahead of him. Peter stopped short. His fingers closed tightly around the handle of his knife. He was certain now that something or someone stood near him, hidden by the thick screen of leaves. He stared uncertainly into the darkness.

Suddenly there was a gleam between the leaves. On the path before him, only a few feet away, stood *Okhanyayo,* the Shining One.

Immediately Peter's fear vanished. He did not move; he scarcely dared to breathe, as for the second time he looked into the huge amber eyes. The little animal regarded him with a wistful melancholy. Peter longed to touch the smooth, shining flanks. Cautiously he moved a step forward and gently held out his hand. With a toss of its head the impala jerked out of reach. Peter felt a surge of disappointment.

Again he stepped forward, but as he did so the impala leaped lightly off the path. Once it flashed briefly at the end of the dark tunnel of trees, then it was gone, swallowed up in the blackness of the night.

The wind sighed in the branches. The whole bush seemed to echo: *Beware—beware.*

Fear gripped Peter, and he ran toward the friendly lights of his house.

DISTURBING NEWS

THE honey bird in the jacaranda tree stared down with interest as Peter assembled a variety of objects at the foot of the garden tree. He laid out two gourds, large flat stones, corn kernels, dried fish, and a shiny green watermelon. The honey bird, unable to understand what was happening, flew off in disgust. Peter continued his preparations for the native banquet to which he had invited his mother.

It was not a very good feast, Peter confessed to himself. He was not at all sure that his mother would like the dried fish—it did smell rather strong. But she had loved the last feast they had eaten together.

He went into the house and returned with a stone jar of grenadilla juice. As he laid it on the ground, a few drops spilled. He watched, fascinated, as numbers of red sugar ants raced to the spot. Within a minute there was no trace of the juice.

Now everything was ready. "The feast is waiting!" Peter called eagerly to his mother. Mrs. Ward came down the garden path, looking cool in her green dress and large straw sun hat.

She knelt down on the cushion Peter had thoughtfully provided and clapped her hands imperiously. "The first course," she cried.

Peter handed her the dried fish. His mother took it and ate it without protest. If she found it unpleasant she gave no sign.

Peter picked up the stones and began to pound the corn kernels, called *mealie*. He was not doing it very successfully. Mrs. Ward watched her son gravely, then said, "Boy, the great white lady would love a piece of watermelon. The corn pleases her not."

Laughing, Peter dropped the stones. He unsheathed his knife and cut into the smooth pink flesh of the watermelon. He handed his mother a slice and took one for himself. It was good! Glancing at his mother, he saw that she was enjoying it too. When they had finished, Peter poured the grenadilla juice into the gourds. Solemnly he handed one to his mother. She accepted it graciously and drained it to the bottom.

"Darling, that was a lovely feast," she said. "Do ask me again."

She got to her feet. Suddenly Peter wanted to tell his mother everything. But something held him back and he merely said, "All right, Mother. I will. Soon."

Mrs. Ward left her son and walked up the lawn. Through the study window she could see her husband bent over his desk. He was so absorbed in his work that he did not see her. Sighing, she turned away.

Hector Ward was worried. He disliked anything that he could not figure out. Years of roaming the bushveldt had given him a great understanding of the ways of the wild creatures. It was an understanding learned slowly and dangerously, over a long period of time. Yet even now, he admitted to himself, he was constantly being surprised.

Of the sudden invasion of the Reserve of thousands upon thousands of impala, he could make nothing. In less than two weeks the impala population had increased a hundredfold, and it was still growing. Where had they all come from? He shook his head and pulled reflectively on his pipe. In all the forty years he had spent in Africa, he had never encountered anything like it.

As he sat at his desk he wished that he could be outside in the sun, but there was work to be done. He sighed and picked up the five letters that lay before him. He read them again. Their contents were curiously similar. They were written by wardens of other reserves in different regions of Africa, but they all told the same strange story.

Great herds of impala were streaming into the reserves. In the past few weeks countless thousands of the creatures had entered, and every day the numbers increased. No letter offered any possible explanation.

A feeling of unease crept over Hector Ward. He rose

from his chair and went over to the window. The garden was peaceful. Old Jabula was asleep beneath a red-flowered Kaffir boom tree, and Peter was stalking an imaginary quarry through the trees.

Mr. Ward watched his son and made a mental note to remind him never to stand against the skyline. Surely the boy knew that he'd be seen a mile away by any self-respecting game!

The sound of a car interrupted his thoughts. He glanced at his watch. Eleven o'clock—time for morning tea. His caller, whoever he was, had timed his visit well.

Hector Ward was not surprised when Richard Hutchison strode in. His famous hat was pulled down over his forehead. The house boy glided in with tea, and the two men sat down.

Without ceremony Hector thrust the opened letters into Richard's hand.

"Read them," he said abruptly. Then, when Richard had finished, he asked, "What do you make of it?"

"I don't begin to understand. I want you to look at something I have here for you."

The caller extracted a crumpled piece of newspaper from a battered wallet and handed it to his host. Under the heading "Great Increase in Game Poaching" Hector Ward read the following:

Alarming reports have been coming in that vast herds of impala in many regions have been illegally slaughtered. The reason for this massacre is entirely unknown. Except in the reserved areas, the impala are now in danger of extinction.

Mr. Ward shook his head sadly. "I don't know what to make of it."

"And the natives tell me," said Richard, "that the poor little devils were left lying where they were shot. Except—except that in almost every case the horns of the impala rams had been removed."

"The horns?" exclaimed Hector Ward. "Why would anyone want the horns? They are of little value—except possibly as trophies. And these hunters scarcely seem like the kind of people interested in sport," he added bitterly.

"The other thing I came over to tell you about is— Philip Keen. Remember him?" Hector Ward nodded and Richard Hutchison went on, "Oddly enough, I've had a letter from him. You know his farm, north of the river, is outside the Reserve, but there is plenty of game there, especially impala. Well, Philip says he has a hunch that there may be an attack on the impala near there in the next few days. Which is Philip's way of letting us know that he has some pretty definite information. Don't ask me how or what . . . that man knows everything . . . he's uncanny."

"Yes," agreed Hector Ward, "he is a strange man. I wouldn't care to live alone there, the way he does."

"You're right," said Richard, "but I don't think he's lonely. I believe he prefers the animals he has to human society."

Mr. Ward laughed, then added thoughtfully, "I think he loves animals more than any man alive."

"I have heard it said," Richard remarked, "that he would stop at nothing to save an animal. That's putting it rather strongly. Still, I think we ought to visit him."

"Yes," Hector Ward agreed. "We will drive there this afternoon. It's too late to let him know we're coming, but he's not the man to worry about that. We'll take Peter along. Mary's been wanting to go to town for a few days and this will give her a chance. We might take Umosogo too; he could be useful."

Hector Ward felt his mood of depression vanish. He threw himself into preparation for the journey. Peter was delighted when he was told they were going to visit Philip Keen. He wondered if Mr. Keen still had his pet monkey.

That afternoon, soon after lunch, Peter and Umosogo climbed into the back seat of the station wagon. Hector Ward and Richard Hutchison sat in front.

Mrs. Ward waved good-by to her family.

"Give my regards to Philip." And as the car drove away she called after it, "Get to bed early, Peter."

MERIBI DRIFT

$\mathcal{A}$T the gate of the Reserve the guard recognized the warden's car and waved it through with a gauntleted hand. Leaving the dirt tracks of the Reserve, the car sped out on a tarred road. Peter, looking ahead, saw it stretch before them in an endless black ribbon. A heat haze shimmered on its hard surface, giving an illusion of wetness.

For many miles Mr. Ward drove steadily on through the monotonous bush country. Ahead was a line of blue mountains. These gave way at last to wide, treeless plains, studded sparsely with aloe trees and cactus standing like great green candlesticks.

It seemed to Peter a long time before they reached the mountains and began the climb up the sharply curving road of the pass.

At the top Mr. Ward stopped the car for a few moments' rest. All four of them climbed out to stretch their legs. Peter paused and looked down on the orange and lemon plantations stretched for miles beneath them, for this was the citrus-growing area. It was blossom time, and as they drove down into the valley the air was full of a faintly bitter, yet fragrant scent.

It was so sultry and airless that the heat seemed like something one could almost touch. As they drove on, the sky changed from a dazzling blue to a sullen gray.

"Looks like a storm," Mr. Ward said a little anxiously. "We must try to be over Meribi Drift before it breaks."

Peter noticed in the west a purple cloud oddly fringed with a dull orange glow. Not a breath of air stirred in the branches of the trees. Mr. Ward pressed his foot on the accelerator, and the car lurched and swayed with the unaccustomed speed. On and on they drove. Above them the sky darkened, and the glow deepened to a fiery red. They were startled by a sudden violent clap of thunder and the blinding flash of the lightning. After a moment's intense silence, the storm clouds burst. The rain fell in a shining, unbroken curtain, shutting out the blue hills and the citrus groves behind its luminous mist.

Above the deafening noise of the thunder Peter heard his father shout, "How far to the river?"

Richard leaned toward him to answer briefly, "About three miles."

The car skidded dangerously on the slippery surface of the road, but Hector Ward was an excellent driver and they kept going without mishap. The rain poured

down unceasingly. As they rounded a sharp bend in the road they came upon a family of wild pigs standing motionless in the waving grass at the road's edge. For a moment Peter glimpsed them dark and wet, their thin tails raised comically against the lashing rain. Then, frightened by the car, they leaped into sudden life and galloped, screeching, along the road.

Mr. Ward slowed the car. "Why don't the stupid creatures turn into the safety of the bush instead of into the narrow road?" he complained. Abruptly the hectic squeals ceased as the largest pig came to his belated senses and led his family off the highway. Mr. Ward shook his head and accelerated.

Richard laughed. "Funny to see them hold their tails up against the storm. Can't be much protection!"

They reached the river and bumped down its sloping banks to the water's edge.

The Drift, like so many bridges in Africa, was merely a concrete causeway. Beneath it were sluices; in normal times these were adequate to take the flow of water. Often the water would rise and spill over the causeway, but it was still perfectly possible to cross the river. Only when the water reached the level of the concrete marker posts on either side of the Drift was crossing dangerous.

The Meribi Drift posts were quite visible. Peter could see them, marking the edge of the Drift, but the rain blotted out his view of the opposite bank.

The two men in the front seat looked ahead. Then Hector Ward spoke. "It looks all right. Shall we risk it? The Drift should be safe enough for a while, provided the water doesn't rise too suddenly with all this rain."

His companion spoke decisively. "The water has not nearly reached the danger level. The longer we wait, the worse our chances are of reaching Blue Wildebeest Farm tonight."

These words seemed to decide Peter's father. Steadily he edged the car into the river. All went well until the car reached the center of the bridge. There all of them could see that there was no time to be lost. The water was rising fast; they would reach the other side with very little time to spare.

Anxiously Mr. Ward pressed the accelerator. The car jerked forward. Then, without warning, the engine spluttered once and died.

In the silence that followed the water sounded very loud in Peter's ears. He sat tensely as his father tried desperately to restart the car. After a moment it coughed into life. Hope soared again, then died as the engine stubbornly refused to start.

"Water on the plugs. She'll never start." Hector Ward sounded grim, but he turned and smiled reassuringly at his son, "We will have to walk it, Pete. We don't want to spend the night in the river." He paused, then continued, "You and I will go first. Richard, bring the guns; Umosogo, take the basket of food. Keep steady, Pete, and all will be well. You can call yourself a true African when you've crossed the river."

"All right," said Peter, rather anxiously.

"Ready, everyone?" called his father.

Already the water was beginning to pile up against

the car on the driver's side. Richard Hutchison and Umosogo wrenched open the doors on the other side.

Helped by his father, Peter stepped carefully into the swiftly flowing, yellow water. The rain hit his face with almost blinding violence. For a moment he shut his eyes against the stinging drops. The current plucked at his knees and he clutched at the car to remain upright. The cement beneath his feet was slimy with green weed. Cautiously he edged forward, pitting his strength against the pull of the current. He took a few more steps, then suddenly he slipped and his hand was wrenched from his father's grasp. For a horrifying moment Peter felt himself being swept toward the edge of the Drift. Another instant and he would have been carried away. Then he felt himself being gripped by the shoulder. Struggling and gasping, he was pulled to his feet by his father's strong arm.

"Steady, Pete."

Peter grasped his father's hand. Together they waded forward. Peter wished that he could see the opposite bank. Surely they must reach it soon. He could see his father peering through the blinding rain and could hear him cursing himself for a fool and saying that they should never have tried to cross. With a shudder, Peter tightened his grip on his father's hand. He could dimly see the others following.

The easy slope of the far side of the Drift loomed up out of the gloom. Thankfully they plunged toward it, praying that the water might rise no higher.

Mr. Ward gained the slope first and pushed Peter up

ahead of him. He turned to shout encouragement to the others. But his words were lost in a terrible, dull roaring sound that every second grew louder. The water from inflowing streams had massed together and the flood was sweeping down in a great wave. Very soon it would be upon them.

Peter heard it, too. "Hurry, Mr. Hutchison! Hurry, Umosogo!" he yelled.

Peter saw the cold swirl of the water rise around Richard Hutchison's waist. He saw him raise the rifles above his head and press frantically against the swift flow of the river. Every second it threatened to lift him off his feet. With a desperate effort he reached the bank and grasped Mr. Ward's outstretched hands. They helped him up the slippery slope to safety, where he staggered and fell from exhaustion.

At that instant Umosogo gave a great cry of terror. Peter looked in fascinated horror as the water whirled the native off the Drift and swept him downstream. Desperately he struck out for the bank, but the current was too strong for him. Fifty yards downstream the water broke into a white foam over jagged rocks, and he was being rushed toward them. Despairingly he still swam. With a superhuman effort he gained a yard toward the bank, where he was swept below an overhanging branch. Umosogo raised a frantic arm and grabbed it. The branch bent, cracked—and held.

All this happened so fast that before Richard had risen to his feet, Peter and his father were off. Leaping over the rocks at the river's edge, they reached the place where Umosogo still clung for his life.

Mr. Ward leaned forward to grasp Umosogo by the hand. Peter had a nightmare vision of his father, rocking and swaying on the very edge of the torrent. He seized him around the waist and steadied him. Together they heaved and strained. For a long moment it seemed as though they could not save Umosogo. Then, with a final superhuman effort, they dragged him from the current's grip and up the bank. Umosogo staggered and fell.

There was a shriek from Richard: "The water!"

In an instant Umosogo was up, and they were all racing for the high ground above the river. Behind them a great wave swept down. It swamped the banks where, only a moment before, they had stood. On it rushed, ripping and tearing at the banks like an angry monster.

Silently they stood and watched. The flood swirled and foamed over the car. For a little while it seemed to withstand the onslaught of the current. Then, inevitably, the force of the water swept it downstream. The roar of the wave died away.

"I was rather fond of that car," said Mr. Ward. He looked so comically sad that Peter burst out laughing. The sound of his laughter broke the tension and the numbing terror passed. It was good to be alive and unhurt. They were all safe, and that was the only thing that mattered.

They were a sorry sight—wet, muddy, and cold. On

his head Richard still wore his hat. He took it off and lovingly pushed it back into shape. Through the thinning rain, the evening sun began to shine warm and golden. The dull brown water sparkled.

"Are you all right, Umosogo?" Mr. Ward asked quietly.

"Yes, *Inkosi*." Umosogo grinned broadly.

Peter gazed at him with admiration. "You are very brave—and very strong, Umosogo," he said.

"It will be dark soon," said Hector Ward. "What we need now is a fire. We may have to spend the night here. At least let's have dry clothes."

His brisk good sense woke them all to a frenzy of activity. On the highest ground above the river they found a deserted kraal. Inside were a few small pieces of dry wood which they heaped outside the enclosure.

"My matches are soaking wet!" Dismayed, Richard tossed them away.

With a smile, a little tinged with smugness, Hector Ward produced a box of matches neatly wrapped in a waterproof cover.

Peter grinned as Richard Hutchison raised his hand in salute.

A few minutes later they had coaxed a flame. Now the fire began to burn and they were able to dry their clothes in its warming glow.

"I'm hungry," said Peter.

"We could have eaten the provisions we brought for Philip," said his father, "but Umosogo could scarcely be expected to hold on to them."

Richard, with the air of a magician pulling a rabbit out of a hat, produced some soggy strips of biltong from his pocket.

Hector Ward laughed. "We're quits," he said.

There was enough for everyone—not a very exciting meal, but a great deal better than nothing.

In the west the sun was sinking, fiery red against the flamingo-colored clouds. The thorn trees were etched black against the sky.

Mr. Hutchison spoke to Umosogo in his native tongue, then translated his answer to the others.

"Umosogo knows a short cut through the bush to Meribi, where we can borrow a car," he told Hector and Peter Ward. "If you two will wait here, I will go with Umosogo, and we'll come back and collect you later."

Hector Ward protested mildly that he ought to be the one to go, but Hutchison was already on his feet, pulling on his dry shirt and ramming the hat fiercely down on his thick hair.

Mr. Ward glanced at his son's white, tired face. "All right," he agreed, "I'll stay with Peter."

In the excitement of the moment, Peter had almost forgotten the object of their journey. Now recollection came flooding back. There was something important to discuss about the impala. They must press on to Blue Wildebeest Farm.

With a cheerful wave of his hand, Richard Hutchison followed Umosogo's tall figure into the darkness.

Peter stared up at the stars. How long would they

have to wait? He wondered where the car was. How far downstream had it been swept by the raging waters?

His father heaped more sticks onto the fire. Peter stared into the blaze until he could no longer fight the sleep that threatened to overwhelm him. Then he lay down on the hard ground, pillowed his head on his hands, and soon drifted into a troubled dream.

For a long time Mr. Ward watched; then he, too, slept. A tiny muskrat gazed curiously at the two motionless figures and scurried past them without fear.

Beneath the slope, the river once more flowed peacefully on its way.

EIGHT

BLUE WILDEBEEST FARM

*W*HEN Peter awoke it was still dark, but he could see that dawn was not far off. He uncurled himself stiffly and lay on his back, looking at the fading stars. Beneath him the ground felt very hard. He sat up and poked idly at the ashes in an attempt to bring the embers to life. His father lay asleep, his pipe still in his hand.

Peter got up quietly and put some sticks on the fire. Small flames sprang up; soon the fire flickered into reluctant life. Slowly the sky lightened and one by one the stars went out. A reed buck whistled shrilly, and Hector Ward stirred restlessly in his sleep.

His hands clasped around his knees, Peter sat by the fire and waited. For a long time he waited. Then, far away, he heard the soft purr of an engine. He stood up and looked down the road. In the distance he saw the flash of headlights. A car was approaching.

As if by some intuition, Peter's father awoke in time to see a large station wagon come around the bend in the road. Peter shouted joyfully, and the car halted. In the uncertain light he ran down the steep slope to greet Hutchison and Umosogo. Hector Ward stamped out the fire and heaped it with earth, then followed his son to the road. Soon the four were speeding north on their interrupted journey to Blue Wildebeest Farm.

"I've left word about your car," Richard spoke cheerfully. "They're sending a boy to look for it—or what's left of it. They'll let us know at Keen's place."

The road was now little more than a rutted track. The car lurched and swayed over the large stones that littered the way. On either side the bush grew sparsely. Tall ant hills rose steeply out of the long grass. Once a mongoose skipped over the road ahead and vanished into the bush.

The sun was now high in the sky. In the back of the car Peter slept fitfully, so that he did not see a large notice on a tree: "Blue Wildebeest Farm," with an excellent drawing of the animal beneath the words. They turned up the long, red, dusty track that led to the farm. Peter sat up just as they drove to the door of a low, rambling, wooden building, with a black corrugated iron roof.

A loud barking greeted their arrival. Two enormous ridgeback dogs bounded around the corner of the house.

They were followed by a pointer that trotted up to investigate the newcomers.

In answer to the barking, the door of the house was flung open. For a moment Philip Keen stood glaring at his visitors. Then a huge smile of recognition and welcome spread over his face. With a shout of pleasure he ran forward and pulled open the door of the car. The occupants climbed stiffly out.

"Richard, by all that's wonderful! And you, too, Hector! What brings you to my humble dwelling?"

"The unique pleasure of your company, Philip," Richard replied impressively.

Keen laughed delightedly. He flung an arm around Peter's shoulders, and led his guests into the house.

In a long, low room Philip Keen splashed out a drink for each of his guests and turned to face them, still smiling broadly.

What a striking man! thought Peter. His tall, spare figure was crowned by a thatch of sunbleached hair, his eyes were a singular light green. Peter noticed how they gleamed, brilliant with excitement, in his angular brown face.

Keen swallowed his drink in one gulp and fired a string of questions. "How long are you going to stay? Why haven't I seen any of you for so long? Where's Mary?"

Hector answered patiently, "Mary is in Johannesburg. We've been rather busy. We'll stay as long as you'll have us."

Then Keen asked the question that Peter had been waiting for. "Have you had anything to eat?"

They replied politely that they had not.

"Great heavens, why didn't you say so before?" In a frenzy of hospitality Philip Keen rushed away to organize a meal. The door slammed behind him with a crash that made the whole house shake.

"Gosh!" said Peter. His father laughed.

Over the meal they recounted their adventures to the excitable Mr. Keen. He listened to their story, interrupting only with an occasional long whistle.

When they had finished he said, "Now, why have you come—really? Nothing to do with my letter, eh, Richard?"

Richard laughed. "Right first time, old boy."

"Look, Philip," asked Hector Ward, "we want to know why you think your farm will be the next target for the poachers."

Philip Keen leaned back in his chair and began. "Last week I heard that there were four men at the trading post. Young Kolo—a boy of mine, and a scoundrel if ever there was one—decided to 'investigate' their jeep. By all accounts he didn't find anything worth stealing, but he saw something which sounds, from the description, very like a machine gun. By the time I heard about it, the strangers had gone. Next day I heard that they were still in the district, so I sent off that letter to you."

"What are we going to do about it?" asked Richard Hutchison.

"I have natives watching all the water holes, with

instructions to come to me if they see anything suspicious. We can't do anything but wait."

After the meal the three men went out on to the stoop to smoke. Peter, thinking over what he had heard, wandered into the hot, bright sunshine.

Behind the house a few sulky-looking hens scratched in the dust. They clucked hysterically as he approached. A lean, yellow Kaffir dog regarded the intruder unpleasantly, but did not move. When Peter bent to stroke it, the dog growled and bared its teeth. A tiny naked native child ran gleefully from the back door and scattered the hens in confusion. The little fellow stopped when he saw Peter and gazed at him with round black eyes.

"Hello," said Peter.

A large Zulu woman swooped down on the child and snatched him away, her intricately patterned bead necklaces swinging indignantly. Peter watched them go with amusement.

In the distance he could see the farm buildings, and he walked toward them. The yard seemed deserted. Only a solitary Shangaan, a battered hat tipped over his eyes, squatted against the barn doors. He did not stir as Peter passed. In the dust more hens flapped energetically in an attempt to bathe their bedraggled plumage.

Peter crossed the yard and went out of the gate that was cunningly made of old wagon wheels. On the other side of the barn he came upon two Basuto.

"*Lumela,*" they greeted him, then went on slowly

unloading a load of mealie from an ox wagon. Peter stopped to stroke the oxen. A crowd of flies crawled on their heads. Peter waved his hand and the flies rose in a buzzing cloud, only to settle again almost immediately.

He turned away and looked across to the corn patches and the green fields of Kaffir corn. Between lay stretches planted with sunflowers. Slowly he turned back toward the house. He looked at Philip Keen's small garden, if it could be called a garden. In the baked earth patches of greenish-gray Kikuyu grass struggled to survive, and a few flower shrubs grew dejectedly.

As Peter passed one of the shrubs, he heard a sudden chattering. A lithe form leaped from the shadows onto his shoulder. He stopped, startled for a moment before he realized that it was Philip Keen's pet monkey. The monkey chewed at a nut. It wound one gray arm around Peter's neck, peering into his face. With the monkey still perched happily on his shoulder, Peter walked up the lawn in front of the house.

As he approached, the three men on the stoop stopped talking. Richard Hutchison yawned loudly. "Look, old boy, what we all need is some sleep. I'm so tired I can't think properly."

Hector Ward laughed and agreed. Only Peter did not think that it was such a good idea.

"Help yourselves to beds," said Philip.

All afternoon the sun blazed down on the silent house. Even the host slept, stretched out in a large chair, two dogs motionless at his feet.

That evening, much refreshed, they sat on the

stoop sipping their drinks and enjoying the pleasant coolness after the heat of the day.

A loud cry rang out in the silence.

"*Inkosi, Inkosi.*"

Startled, they jumped to their feet. A native boy, running at full speed, was rounding the corner of the house. The next instant he was at the stoop, his breath coming in great gasps. Beads of sweat trickled from his shining black face.

"*Inkosi,*" he cried again.

"What is it, Jakopo?" his master asked.

"White men!" Jakopo answered breathlessly. "White men with guns, *Inkosi*. White men shooting."

"Who saw them, Jakopo?"

"Kaloba, *Inkosi*. Kaloba, he see them!"

"My goodness, Richard! Kaloba was watching Nsingozo Water Hole. It's the one nearest the farm. The impudent devils!"

Philip turned to the others, his face ablaze with determination, and barked out orders: "Richard, you get our guns. Hector, you had better find Umosogo. I'll go for the car."

Without question they obeyed.

The car drew up with a screech of brakes in front of the stoop. Richard and Hector and the two native boys leaped in. In the hurry, no one thought to argue with Peter, so he came too.

They drove off. "Where is Kaloba?" Philip flung over his shoulder to the still-panting Jakopo.

"Kaloba, he at my kraal, *Inkosi*."

"It's on our way," shouted Philip. He swung the car violently to the right, hurling everyone off balance, though he did not seem to notice.

The track to Jakopo's kraal was very rough. The car swayed and jolted, but the driver bent over the wheel and drove ever faster.

They reached the kraal, and Kaloba ran to meet them. Behind him a little knot of women and children stood and watched cautiously. Philip leaned out and spoke quickly to Kaloba in his own language. Kaloba answered, pointing in the direction of the river. Philip ordered him into the car. Then he raced on, his foot hard down on the accelerator. Behind them rose a great cloud of red dust, churned up by the spinning wheels of the car.

Umosogo said something in a low voice to Kaloba and Jakopo. Philip Keen, glancing into the driving mirror, saw his two boys staring fixedly at Peter, who had not seen their gaze. Philip frowned suddenly and looked away.

With Kalobo as guide, they made good progress. "Not far from Nsingozo now," Philip shouted above the frantic roar of the engine. As he spoke, the wheel wrenched itself from his grasp. Desperately he tried to steady the wildly skidding vehicle. It slewed around on the track and came to a sudden stop, its hood buried in the branches of a thorn tree.

They all jumped out. Almost at once they saw what they had feared was true—on the near front side the tire was flat as a pancake. Philip shouted orders to his boys. They got out the spare tire and tools and began to jack up the car.

Suddenly a series of shots shattered the tense silence. "Quick!" yelled Keen. "To the river. Follow me."

Seizing his rifle from the car, he set off at breakneck speed. The men ran after him. The native boys dropped the tools and ran too.

"Keep behind me, Peter," warned Mr. Ward.

Philip Keen ran like a deer. He knew every inch of the country. He swooped and bent to avoid the branches that overhung the path. His green eyes blazed in his brown face, and he scarcely noticed the pace at which he ran. In the heat of his anger he had momentarily forgotten the others. They were a little distance behind and were finding it rough going.

Two or three gray louries, warning birds of the bush, shrieked their warning: *Go away—go away—go away.* Their tails jerked with the effort.

Now the men had reached the slopes that led down to the river. The going was easier here. Suddenly Philip slowed down. He signaled back to the others to move with caution. "Quiet," he whispered.

Ahead the bush was thinning. Silently the party crept toward the clearing, rifles at the ready. When they had moved forward until only a few flat-topped thorn bushes stood between them and the clearing, they halted to peer through the network of branches.

Peter looked with horrified eyes at the scene of devastation before them. No living thing stirred in the green silence. All around lay dead impala, ruthlessly slaughtered as they had fled in terror from the river. They lay now as they had fallen, their sad, dark eyes turned in a mute condemnation of their murderers.

With something like a sob, Philip Keen knelt down beside one of them and touched the still form.

The killers, warned by the louries, seemed to have made their escape. Suddenly the silence was shattered by the sound of an engine being started.

With a hoarse yell of fury, Philip Keen straightened up, darted across the clearing and into the bush beyond. The others followed on his heels.

They had not far to go. A few hundred yards farther on they came to another large space. At the edge of it a small car was moving slowly away. They were too late!

But as the car started Peter had a glimpse of one of its occupants. It was the red-bearded man that he had met that day in the Rest Camp!

Dazed by what they had seen, they turned back. They stopped again at the place where the dead impala lay. Now they noticed that the horns of some of the impala were missing. Bewildered, they stared at each other.

THE LEGEND

LATE that night Peter, his father, and Richard sat around Philip Keen's fireplace. Outside a misty rain fell softly.

Philip Keen entered the room. He walked without his usual vigor and his face was set. The others made room for him and he slumped wearily into his chair.

There was no light in the room except for the fire, which flickered eerily among the shadows. As Peter watched, the flames suddenly leaped up. The impala head on the wall glowed red and the fixed glass eyes seemed almost lifelike. Peter turned his head away.

Switching on a table lamp, Philip Keen opened the newspaper and began to read. Peter noticed that his eyes kept straying absently from the printed pages.

Hector Ward began to scribble on a scrap of paper a report of the day's events.

Richard Hutchison continued to stare listlessly into the fire. Peter whittled miserably at a piece of wood.

With an impatient gesture Philip Keen tossed the paper aside, stood up, and walked over to the window. He looked out moodily and, with his back to the others, he asked, "Have you ever heard the legend of the Golden Impala?"

Peter stiffened warily.

"No. Tell us about it," Mr. Ward suggested.

Philip returned to the fire and drew up his chair. The others, including Peter, listened intently.

"Long, long ago, at the beginning of time, the impala were not as you and I know them now. They were golden and shone like the sun that beat down on the hot African plains where they roamed at will. For thousands of years the impala's only enemies were the lion and the leopard, the lynx and the wild dog. Then man came and coveted their beautiful shining skins. He hunted them so remorselessly that there might have been none left. But the Spirit of the Bush, who loved the impala, changed them into the color which they are today. Now you can see the faint gleam that is all that is left of their once golden coats only when the sun shines.

"The Spirit changed them all—all, that is, save one. It decreed that in every generation a single Golden Impala would be born. This Golden Impala would never be seen by man, save in a time when a great peril should threaten the impala race. Then this Golden Impala, which the natives call *Okhanyayo,* the Shining One, would appear and would lead all its kind to safety."

Hector Ward frowned. "Lead them to safety?" He stopped, as an idea began to form in his mind. "I wonder . . ." he began hesitatingly.

"Well?" said Philip abruptly.

Choosing his words carefully, Hector Ward went on. "It's a funny thing that for the past week or so the reserves have been invaded by vast numbers of impala."

"Impala? Only impala?" Philip asked, though his tone sounded almost as if he knew the answer.

"Yes. It's almost like a mass migration. But why? Why?"

"And what's more," broke in Richard, "it's not only in our reserve, but in all the others as well!"

"It must be a coincidence," said Mr. Ward firmly.

"You sound very sure of yourself," said Philip Keen. Then he added, very low, "Odd things have happened in Africa."

"Perhaps," said Mr. Ward doubtfully. "But that legend is pretty hard to believe."

"You haven't heard the whole of it yet," said Philip.

"Go on," said Peter quickly.

Philip continued. "You remember I said that the Golden Impala was destined to save its race? But," said Philip with emphasis, "it can do this only with the aid of a white boy."

Peter spoke urgently. "What must the white boy do?"

"I don't know," said Philip. "The natives are very secretive about this part of the story. All I know is that they call this boy *Okhethiwe*, the Chosen."

"*Okhethiwe,* the Chosen." Peter repeated the words softly.

Hector Ward laughed. "It's only a legend, Peter. Don't go imagining yourself to be *Okhethiwe.*"

The others grinned. Peter flushed.

"Who is this white boy, anyway?" Mr. Ward asked.

"The natives know, but they won't say," Philip told him.

Richard sounded skeptical. "A boy could never keep a secret like that."

For a fleeting instant Peter's eyes met Philip's. Deliberately Philip replied, "The Golden Impala can never succeed, unless the boy keeps silent."

Peter's knife slipped from his fingers and fell to the **floor.**

MISSING

*T*HE next day word was brought that Mr. Ward's car had been found farther downstream, a total wreck.

Philip offered to drive his visitors home. Leaving the borrowed car to be picked up, they set off at midday in his car. The road was now very dry. Clouds of red dust rose from beneath their wheels, blotting out their last sight of Blue Wildebeest Farm. Several times they had to come to an abrupt halt and wait for the trail of dust from a passing car to clear before they could see their way to go on.

At length they reached Meribi Drift. The raging torrent of two nights before was now a peaceful river, but heaps of shattered trees and rushes marked where the wave had passed.

Philip stopped the car at the edge of the Drift. The

yellow water slid smoothly over the concrete surface. A family of dabchicks swam away upstream. A fish flashed in a glittering arc. Dragon flies swooped and darted over the water's surface.

Not far off, three hippo played contentedly in the river, blowing noisily and calling to each other. Peter watched them submerge their great leather bodies for a long time, then rise slowly to the surface, appearing little by little above the water. They acted, Peter thought, as if they were afraid that the world might have altered in some disturbing way since before their dive. But nothing had changed, and all was peaceful.

"We were very lucky," said Mr. Ward grimly. Umosogo shivered. They drove on, the water swirling lightly around their wheels. A few glistening bubbles floated downstream.

Once over the Drift, Philip drove swiftly. All of them were impatient to reach the Ward home before darkness fell.

Sometimes a native child would run to the side of the road and hold out a chubby black palm, hoping for a penny or a piece of candy. A native dressed in a pair of brilliantly striped pajamas and a straw hat came swaying unsteadily along on a bicycle. As they sped past, Peter waved gaily. Unable to wave back, the native grinned hugely. They rounded a corner and the gay figure was lost from view. Soon Peter saw a native postman racing along the road, holding aloft a letter in a cleft stick.

In the trees that boarded the edge of the road, starlings fluttered. White tick birds stalked imperiously out of the long grass. Peter loved their air of dignity.

A few hours later they entered the Reserve. Gladly the dust-stained travelers tumbled out of the car and into the house.

Mr. Ward was almost relieved to find that his wife had not yet returned from Johannesburg. He hated to tell her about the car; now there was no immediate need. She had sent word that she was going to stay in Johannesburg for several more days. Hector asked Philip to stay on and, to his surprise, Philip accepted.

As the days passed, fresh reports of illegal slaughter of the impala reached the warden's house. Peter watched his father become more grim and silent, though on the day of his wife's return he seemed in better spirits.

After breakfast that day Philip drove off with Mr. Ward and Peter to meet Mrs. Ward. At the gate of the Reserve the warden got out to speak to the rangers, who saluted him respectfully. As a precaution he had increased the number of rangers and ordered a more detailed search of all cars entering the Reserve. But everything was as usual. As he went into the rangers' hut he noticed Peter's anxious face. "It's all right, Peter," he said. "We are in good time."

Peter soon saw proof of his father's efficiency. A large station wagon, painted a hideous bright yellow, drove through the entrance gate and halted. In it sat two men. As always, a ranger came out to attend to them. The men paid for the tickets which permitted them to drive in the Reserve and stay at the many rest camps. The driver of the car then handed out a small bore rifle, which was duly sealed by the ranger and returned to its owner, with the stern warning that if the seal were broken the penalty would be severe—a stiff fine or three months' hard labor.

The two men smiled broadly and started to drive off. But the ranger stopped them and indicated that he wished to search the car. Peter watched, fascinated, as the vehicle was unloaded. Cameras, bedding and camping equipment for use in rest camps were laid on the ground, together with a large can of milk and food of all kinds.

Satisfied, the ranger helped the two men pile their belongings back in the car. He waved them off with a further warning that it was against the law of the Reserve to get out of one's car. The smaller of the two paused to wipe the dust from his thick-lensed glasses.

Mr. Ward came out of the rangers' hut, and soon the three were speeding along the road to the railway station.

The train was on time. Mrs. Ward stepped out and greeted her husband. He went cheerfully to collect the luggage while Peter hugged his mother. She handed him a mysteriously bulky parcel.

"A present for you, darling," she said.

Peter took it delightedly. Unwrapping the paper, he found a magnificent black flashlight, shaped like a gun. He pressed the trigger and the beam shone, though only faintly in the hard yellow sunlight.

Mrs. Ward greeted Philip warmly. "Where's our car?" she asked as they drove off.

"I'm afraid we had a slight accident," her husband replied. Then he told her the story of their adventures in the Meribi Drift and at Blue Wildebeest Farm.

"Thank God you are all safe," she said quietly when he had finished. Hector changed the subject, asking his wife about her visit. She mentioned shopping, going to the theater, and a dinner party.

"I sat next to a Professor Hardy who was in a terrible state about some stolen papers," she said. "Apparently he had been away for a month and when he returned they were gone. Nothing else was touched."

"What were the papers about?" asked Peter.

"I forgot exactly," his mother answered. "I think he had found some little gland or other and was doing some sort of experimenting with it."

"Poor old professor," said Mr. Ward. "But I can't see why any thief would want papers of that kind."

His wife laughed. "He's probably mislaid them," she said. "Just an absent-minded professor."

They came back into the Reserve, and Philip slowed the car to the speed limit of twenty miles an hour. On either side of the road they glimpsed huge herds of impala. Some three miles from the house they rounded a sharp bend in the road and Mr. Ward gave a loud exclamation of disgust. For there, in the center of the track, stood the yellow car. Both doors were open wide, while its two occupants stood carelessly at the edge of the road erecting their complicated camera apparatus.

Philip drew up short.

"Look here, gentlemen," Mr. Ward shouted angrily, "you were told at the gates that you must stay in your car. These rules are not made for fun, you know. Please get back into your car and do not leave it again, or you will find yourself in trouble."

The men started to argue.

Furiously Hector Ward interrupted them. "Do as I say, and don't let me catch you again. Or I will turn you out of the Reserve altogether, as I have the power to do."

Muttering ungraciously, the two men got into their car and drove off.

"Darned fools," growled Hector Ward.

That day, after tea, Peter was in the garden while the Wards and Philip Keen sat on the stoop behind the green screen of wisteria creeper. The telephone rang in the hall and Mr. Ward answered it.

"That was the Main Gate on the phone," Peter heard him say when he returned. "A car has been found empty near Ibubesini Water Hole and there is no sign of the occupants. The ranger said it was bright yellow."

"It must be the one we saw this afternoon," exclaimed Philip.

The warden sighed. "More than likely," he said. "Those two fools looked capable of anything. They probably got out of the car again to photograph something. That's a bad area for lions, and I dread to think what might have happened. I have to meet the rangers up there. They tried to phone Richard, but he's on his way to Maluza. He goes regularly twice a week."

"What is Maluza?" Philip asked.

"It's a new Rest Camp near Ibubesini Water Hole," said Mr. Ward. "I'll have to leave now," he added, pulling on his jacket that had hung at the back of his chair.

"I'll come with you," cried Philip.

Peter rounded the corner of the house just as the car sped off down the drive.

"Wait for me," he called. "Wait!" But they did not hear him. Disappointed, he trailed into the house.

At Ibubesini Water Hole, some thirty miles away, the search for the missing men continued without result. An empty film carton was found a little distance from the car. Of the occupants there was no sign. Every available ranger was spread out through the bush in that area to the very edge of the Reserve. Soon a message was passed to the warden that tracks of two men had been found. They had apparently climbed over the Reserve fence and disappeared into the bush beyond.

"What do you make of that?" asked Philip.

"Ask me another," said Mr. Ward.

At that moment there was a long hoot on a car horn, and Richard Hutchison drove up, waving furiously.

Startled, they ran toward his car.

"Main Gate has just phoned me," he yelled. "Shots —shots near Thabankwe, Hector, toward Rabi Ford. Got here as quickly as I could. You and Philip go and see if Mary and Peter are all right. I'll get some rangers together here and go directly to the ford."

Philip and Hector drove home as fast as the corrugated road would let them. As they rounded the last bend in the drive, Mrs. Ward ran to meet them. Even in the fierce white glare of the headlights Hector saw that she was deathly pale.

"Peter!" she gasped. "Is he with you?"

As she spoke, she gazed frantically through the car window. Mr. Ward threw open the door and leaped out.

"He's gone," Mrs. Ward told her husband. "Peter's gone! I hoped he was with you."

Old Jabula stepped from the shadows. "Jabula see Master Peter go," he said.

Mr. Ward swung round on the old man. "Which way, Jabula?"

For answer, the old man pointed into the bush in the direction of the water hole near the Umsinsi Rest Camp.

"When, Jabula? When did the young master go?"

With maddening slowness the old man replied, "Guns, *Inkosi*. Many guns. *Nkosana* hear them. He go."

"But that's an hour ago," broke in Philip.

"Come on, Philip," shouted Mr. Ward. "After him!"

They dashed through the garden and into the bush beyond. Mrs. Ward stared after them.

Unexpectedly Old Jabula spoke. "*Nkosana* not alone," he said. "Umosogo, he follow."

Mrs. Ward relaxed a little. "Go after them, Jabula," she cried. "Quickly! Tell that to your master."

Jabula shambled off into the night.

Alone, Mrs. Ward searched the garden once more. But to her repeated calls there was no reply. Far away in the bush a lion roared. The sound rolled and thundered in the still night air. Fearful thoughts crowded in on her. Blindly she ran back into the house and up the stairs to Peter's room. She touched the switch, and light flooded the empty room. She sank down on the bed and buried her head in her hands.

Fighting for control, Mrs. Ward began to tidy the bedside table. She picked up an old, faded sheet of newspaper and was about to crush it in her hands when she noticed that one of the paragraphs was roughly marked with a red pencil. She began to read it aloud.

In order to conduct a series of experiments, the eminent zoologist Professor Hardy . . .

Mrs. Ward stopped. That's odd, she thought. That was the little man at Helen's dinner party. She read on. Vaguely she sensed some connection between this and the slaughter of the impala—but what? And how was Peter caught up in it? Terror gripped her, and again she buried her head in her hands.

PETER ALONE

*A*FTER his father and Philip Keen had left without him, Peter wandered about the house unhappily. He tried to talk to his mother. He tried to read. But he could think only of the thousands of dead impala he had seen—and the Shining One, the Golden Impala.

When he heard the shots, Peter stood for a moment stunned. He realized that the hunters had finally dared to kill in the reserve itself. His father would, by now, be at Ibubesini Water Hole. What could he—Peter—do? If he could only spy on the poachers and track them to their hiding place!

Avoiding his mother, he snatched his new flashlight from the table, ran swiftly through the garden and into the bush.

The shots, he judged, had come from the direction of the Umsinsi Rest Camp. He hurried along the track,

and for a while he made good progress. A stick cracked behind him and he whirled around to face the possible danger, but there was nothing there. A monkey stared at him with bright black eyes and chattered derisively.

Bravely Peter pressed on. A secretary bird in black-feathered tailcoat and hunched shoulders strutted along the path ahead of him. The bird kept its distance, silently stalking on ahead. Then unexpectedly it turned off the track and strutted away into the bush. Peter felt more alone than ever. He glanced up at the darkening sky and saw a little way ahead a spinning cloud of vultures. He must be near the scene of the slaughter. He began to move with great caution.

Again something rustled behind him, closer this time. He stopped, his heart hammering wildly. Ahead, the vultures loomed very near. Jackals, scenting blood, howled excitedly.

Peter glanced over his shoulder, certain that he was being followed. Gripping his flashlight firmly, he crept forward as cautiously as he knew how along the track bordered by tall elephant grass. The bush seemed infinitely large and infinitely dark.

Suddenly a long black arm emerged from the grass and gripped Peter's shoulder. Peter screamed and dropped his flashlight, struggling against the grip. A black face, hideously scarred with Shangaan tribal marking, bent toward him. The native raised his head and whistled softly. Immediately there was an answering whistle.

The native broke into a run, forcing his prisoner on.

The next instant they burst through a screen of bushes into a clearing. Peter had a confused impression of many people, of dead impala, and the great red-bearded man looming up before him. Then something struck him violently on the head. Earth and sky swayed together, and all was darkness.

When Richard Hutchison and the rangers reached the clearing, no human being was in sight.

In silence they surveyed the scene of desolation and death. Richard directed a search for any traces which would lead them to the poachers. A ranger, hunting through the bushes, found Peter's flashlight and brought it to Richard Hutchison.

Richard was still holding it when Hector and Philip dashed into the clearing. Silently he handed the flashlight to his friend.

"It's Peter's," said Mr. Ward. Mechanically he repeated the words, "It's Peter's."

Richard Hutchison touched him gently on the arm. "Steady, old man," he said gently. "We'll find Peter somehow."

The rangers were grouped uncertainly at the entrance to the clearing. They whispered nervously among themselves. Philip glanced toward them as they parted to make way for Jabula. The two wardens turned and saw the old man. There was a hush.

"You find *Nkosana?*" he asked Philip Keen in an expressionless voice.

"No," said Philip. For an instant their eyes met.

"So it must be," said the old man. "He is alone now for good or for ill."

Bewildered, Mr. Ward started forward.

Old Jabula raised his hand slowly. *"Nkosana,* he *Okhethiwe,"* he told his master. *"Nkosana,* he *Okhethiwe,"* he repeated softly.

THE CAVE

*N*o one had seen Umosogo slip silently into the water at the river's edge. No one had seen him grasp the short length of rope that dangled from the second of the two dugouts bearing the kidnapers and the unconscious boy. Now Umosogo clung desperately to the rough rope as the canoes sped down the Nokantsu River. It was dark, for clouds flitting across the sky hid the moon.

Behind the canoe Umosogo was swept first one way and then another by the force of the current. The numbing pain in his arms grew worse, and time and again the rope was nearly ripped from his grasp. His ears were full of the roar of the river and he was half choked by the water. But he would not admit defeat. Was he not Umosogo, son of Kala, the Mighty Hunter? Where the *Nkosana* went, there must Umosogo follow. He clung tenaciously to the thin strand that cut ever more deeply into his hands, and prayed that the crocodiles would not see him and that his strength would not fail.

The two natives, paddling the second canoe, were unaware of their extra burden. Beneath their feet the impala horns rattled dully.

Ahead, in the larger craft, the great red *Inkosi* looked up at the sky. The first pale streaks of dawn appeared. "Hurry!" he urged his companion. "We must reach the cave as soon as possible. After dawn the hue and cry will be on after that boy." He glanced down at the unconscious Peter.

"He knows too much," he remarked grimly. He swung his paddle faster through the water; as if it were a signal, the natives in the second canoe did the same.

Umosogo felt the sudden increase in speed. He was jerked forward so that the rope was all but torn from his grasp. He swung sharply inward; his foot struck a submerged rock with such violence that he cried out with the pain of it. But his shriek was lost in the roar of the water.

He was fast approaching the limit of his strength. Very soon he must let go and be swept relentlessly downstream. If he escaped being dashed to pieces on the rocks, he would be devoured by the waiting crocodiles.

Umosogo flung his head clear of the water; his senses reeled, and a terrible shuddering cold swept up his body.

At that moment the canoe slowed and swung sharply to the left. Again the rope jerked as the canoe turned crosswise in the current. In that brief second Umosogo had tightened his failing grip. Somehow he clung on. The pull of the current slackened, and he felt his foot touch a smooth edge of rock. In the next moment, the roar of the water sounded strangely hollow and distant. They had turned into a narrow tunnel in the rock which barely showed above the level of the river. At the end of the tunnel was a rough mooring place with a wooden ladder stretched up the smooth black wall of the rock.

The canoe stopped. Hastily Umosogo submerged his body until only the tip of his nose showed above the water.

Up the ladder went the occupants of the canoes. First went the leader of the gang, hoisting Peter over one shoulder. The others followed, each carrying a load of impala horns. At the top of the ladder they disappeared into a narrow passage. Umosogo could see them pick their way carefully along it with the help of flashlights.

When Peter recovered consciousness he was lying on the floor not far from a fire. He could see two Shangaans, one of them the much-scarred individual who had captured him. They were soon joined by the tall red-bearded man and a wiry, dark fellow that he had not seen before. Peter's head ached badly. He lay still, pretending to be asleep but listening to the conversation. The dark man, whose name appeared to be Max, addressed his companion.

"No sign of Jake and Steiger yet, Leroux."

"I hope to heaven they haven't been caught," said Leroux. "I was a fool to send Karl to meet them. He might give everything away. He's very jumpy about this whole affair."

"Nevertheless," said Max, "that was a very clever idea of yours to send those two to draw off old Ward and his rangers. You couldn't mistake that yellow car in a hurry."

Leroux smiled and spoke with evident pride.

"That was a good scheme," he said. "And well-timed, so that Hutchison was out of the way."

So that was it, thought Peter. The two men in the yellow car had been a decoy to draw his father from the poachers' trail.

The two Shangaans stood up, in answer to a sharp command from their leader. They shuffled off down the narrow passage that led back to the canoes. As soon as they were out of sight, Leroux leaned forward and said something to his companion. He spoke so low that Peter could make out only two words, though he strained to hear. "Convenient accident," were those two words, and his blood ran cold with fear.

"Come, Max," said Leroux. "I want to see what progress has been made." He turned and started across the cave floor.

"The boy," urged Max. "What about the boy? You can't leave him unguarded."

"Bring him," the other replied shortly.

"He'll see everything," Max complained.

Leroux chuckled mirthlessly. "It won't matter for long," he said.

Fighting down his fear, Peter walked unsteadily along beside Max. Their footsteps echoed eerily and their giant shadows flickered on the walls. At the far end of the cave was a dark, narrow passage. In silence they groped along it toward a faint light which glimmered ahead, guiding them on.

Peter's heart beat fast. In spite of the danger he knew he was in, he was excited at what he was about to see. He felt certain that it would show the reason that lay behind all this strange cruelty and death.

They reached the end of the passage and the entrance to a small cave. It was lighted by paraffin burners that stood on a rough table in the center of this inner cave. On the table, arranged in careful rows, were many slim glass test tubes. Each of them held something that was a pale chalky color. Fascinated, Peter moved to the table, as if to pick up one of the test tubes.

"No!" Max snatched at his wrist in a grip so tight that Peter stifled a cry of pain.

"Do not touch, boy!" he snapped.

"Aren't these ready yet?" Leroux spoke with ill-concealed impatience. He stood with his arms folded, staring down at the table.

Max shook his head. "I need more time."

"How much longer must I wait?" snarled Leroux.

For answer his companion darted over to a corner of the cave. His hands searched the rough wall until he found a loose piece of stone which he pulled away.

There was a cleft in the rock into which Max eagerly put his hand and lifted out a large black box. His fingers fumbled nervously as he sought to open it. Then with a triumphant gesture he swung back the lid.

Astounded, Peter started forward. The box was entirely filled with pearls! Pearls white as milk, their pale moon-shimmer luminous in the flickering light. Pearls of a size undreamed of, flawless, and gleaming, a fabulous fortune in a black box!

With a hoarse cry of pleasure Leroux plunged his hands into the box. He seized great handsful of pearls and let them slide through his fingers. Unnoticed by the two men, one of the pearls fell to the ground and rolled toward Peter. He bent swiftly, snatched it up, and thrust it deep into his pocket. Still laughing triumphantly, Leroux leaned toward his prisoner. "Like to see how it's done?" he crowed exultantly. "Show him, Max. Show him!"

Without taking his eyes from the boy's pale face, Max began to speak. It sounded as if he were reading from a textbook or reciting something he knew by heart. "Pearls are no more than the common chemical calcium carbonate," he said. "Myriads of microscopic crystals, layer upon layer, go to form the smooth surface of a pearl." He paused, then asked Peter, "You are wondering no doubt why, if it is as simple as I have described, no one has succeeded in making pearls long before this?"

"Yes," Peter agreed. "That's exactly what I was wondering."

Pleased with the effect of his words, Max went on. "The wonder of a pearl lies in the way the crystals are laid down. Man can grow these crystals, but he cannot control their arrangement—only the oyster can do this. For thousands of years man has dreamed of discovering something that will imitate the oyster's miraculous chemical powers. He has searched in vain—until now the talented Professor Hardy has discovered a gland at the base of the horn of the impala which contains a secretion from which the liquid man so much desires can be made." Max turned toward Leroux. "A pity the professor was so careless with his papers—but lucky for us, Leroux." The two men laughed loudly.

"We have the secretion," Max went on, proudly, "and we can make pearls large or small, of any color we choose. No one can tell the difference from the real thing, even with the most complicated instruments in the world. And the reason is that this *is* the real thing— it's as simple as that!"

Peter went slowly to the table and this time Max did not stop him. He looked closely at the test tubes, one by one. In each, gradually forming in the pale liquid, grew a single pearl. Behind Peter, Max spoke. "The longer they are left in the tube, the larger they grow."

Peter picked up a large phial half filled with a colorless liquid.

"Take care." Leroux laid a hand on his arm. "That's valuable stuff, boy, and not so easy to obtain."

Peter thought suddenly of all the pain and death that had gone to make this liquid which looked as harmless as water, and his hands shook as he laid down the phial. He thought back to the time when he had first read in the faded newspaper of the professor's experiments. He remembered how he had heard, without making the connection, his mother's story of the theft of the papers. Now, too late, the last piece of the jigsaw had fitted dramatically into place.

"So now you know all," Leroux was saying boastfully, yet with an unmistakable note of menace.

Peter felt a chill creep over him. Yes, he knew all. He knew the secret of the fabulous fortune that lay softly gleaming in the black box. He turned to stare at his captors and he was very frightenend.

THIRTEEN

UMOSOGO

*U*MOSOGO waited for a long time in the clear water behind the canoe. Then, sure that the way was clear, he dragged himself painfully up over its side. He felt half dazed with exhaustion and the chill of the water.

Shivering, Umosogo pulled over himself an old blanket he found in the bottom of the boat. He lay low, hoping desperately that no one would see him. Soon he fell into an exhausted sleep.

When he awoke it was evening. He lay still, wondering what he should do next. Footsteps sounded above him, and before he could move two men appeared above the ladder. The next instant he heard them climb swiftly down, talking as they came. They were Shangaans, and Umosogo could barely understand what they were saying. He pressed his aching body lower and lower onto the hard, damp planks.

For what seemed to Umosogo an eternity, the two Shangaans stood arguing about which canoe to take. From their conversation it was evident that they were being sent to meet someone.

In an agony Umosogo waited while the two men hesitated. If they chose his canoe all was lost. Finally they chose the larger craft, jumped in, and cast off. They passed so close that Umosogo felt that they must surely see him, but they did not. In a moment they were gone, and the swish of their paddles was lost in the roar of the river.

He must find another hiding place, Umosogo decided. To stay any longer where he was meant certain discovery.

He climbed out of the canoe and up the ladder. Stealthily he crept along the passage, until he heard the murmur of voices. He stopped and went back. His hands explored the sides of the passage for a hiding place. Stretching his arms up, his fingers felt the edge of a narrow ledge of rock. If he could haul himself onto it, he would be safe until the time came when he could help his young master. His arms were unbelievably muscular and powerful. Not for nothing had Umosogo practiced the art of assagai throwing as a boy! He pulled himself upward onto the ledge, which was just wide enough to take his body.

After a short time the two Shangaans returned with

three men. Umosogo glared down on them fiercely as they passed only a foot or so below him.

It was nearly midnight when, satisfied that all was quiet, he swung himself off the ledge and began to creep noiselessly up the dark passage.

At the entrance to the cave, Umosogo crouched down behind a great boulder. Around the dying embers of the fire the poachers lay asleep. At first Umosogo could not see Peter. Then his eyes found him, huddled on a blanket a little distance from the fire. He stirred and cried out in his sleep. The native guard who crouched near the fire stood up and leaned over him, fingering the sharp blade of his small ax in his hand. Behind the rock, Umosogo prepared to spring, his lips drawn back over his teeth in a terrifying, though silent, snarl. But the guard, apparently satisfied that the boy was sleeping, straightened up and looked around.

Umosogo felt the ground at his feet. He ran his fingers exploringly behind him and found a small, round pebble. Swiftly he hurled it toward the cave. It fell with a sharp clatter at the dark entrance to the inner cave. The guard whirled around toward the sound; he gripped his ax more firmly, but did not move away from the fire. Umosogo smiled scornfully. He picked up a second pebble and threw it high into the air. It fell in the same place as the first one. This time the guard, ax in hand, glided across the floor of the cave and disappeared into the narrow passage.

This was the opportunity which Umosogo wanted. Silently as a snake he slid out from behind the rock, sprang lightly across the floor, and seized the sleeping boy in his arms. He placed one great hand over Peter's mouth to stifle his cries.

The next instant Umosogo was out of the cave and running silently down the narrow passage that led to the canoes. Peter stirred and opened his eyes. Umosogo looked down into the boy's pale, strained face. "No speak, *Nkosana*," he whispered.

Peter understood. Dimly he wondered how Umosogo had found him.

At the top of the ladder Umosogo set Peter down. For a moment the boy stood swaying, almost falling, then, setting his will to work, he forced himself to follow his rescuer down the ladder and into the small canoe.

A loud shout, followed by a shot, echoed up the passage. Peter knew that already their escape was discovered and the hunt was on. Swiftly Umosogo cast off the canoe, pausing only to loose the other one and so make pursuit impossible. With a rapid, deft movement of the paddle he propelled the canoe through the tunnel and out into the open river, where the current took it.

After the dank atmosphere of the cave, the night air was sweet. Above, stars glittered and the moon shone brilliantly. Free at last, exulted Peter. Free and gliding to safety along a silver river! Exhilarated, he grasped a paddle and struck out boldly. With every yard they moved away from the cave his spirits soared higher.

By an unlucky chance the second canoe, floating out toward the river, had been caught fast by its moorings in a cleft of rock. There the pursuers found it. Quickly they climbed into it and set off after their prisoners.

Peter's joy turned to dismay when he saw the pursuing canoe. Urged on by greater strength, it gained on them with appalling speed. For the moment they were out of range of the guns, but not for long. In the bright moonlight there was no hope of hiding on the river. Their only chance lay in taking to the bush, where they might lose their pursuers among the tangled thorn trees. But every moment the canoe gained on them.

"Hurry, Umosogo!" gasped Peter. "Hurry!"

As they rounded a bend in the river, Umosogo sent the canoe whirling in toward the bank. Peter leaped out; Umosogo followed. Together they climbed for dear life up the steep rocks that bordered the river. Just as they reached the top, the second canoe rounded the bend. With a yell of fury, Leroux saw that his escaped prisoner was already ashore. For a brief instant he saw two figures silhouetted on the crest of the rocks, then they vanished into the bush.

"They shall not escape us now!" cried Leroux, as he flung himself ashore.

For Peter and Umosogo the going was difficult, for the thick bush often barred their way. Sometimes crawling, sometimes running, they pressed on without stopping. The sounds of the pursuers died away into the darkness behind them.

On and on Peter and Umosogo went, but Peter's steps were growing slower. Often he staggered and almost fell. His knees were bleeding where the thorns had torn them; his clothes were ripped in a hundred places.

Beads of sweat ran down his mud-stained face. At last he stumbled and fell exhausted to the ground. There he lay panting, his breath coming in great gasps.

Anxiously, Umosogo bent over him. He saw that his young master could go no farther. Out of the darkness came a sudden, whooping sound. Once more the hunters were close on their track. Peter heard it and dragged himself painfully to his feet. He broke into a halting run.

Nearer and ever nearer came the eerie, whooping call. Umosogo stopped and looked around. Then he gave a little grunt of satisfaction. Seizing Peter, he half carried him toward a bush overhung with creeper and long swathes of interlaced monkey rope. Near the ground was a tiny opening, through which Peter crawled with difficulty. Inside it was very dark; no shaft of moonlight penetrated the green blackness. Here indeed was a safe hiding place.

"*Nkosana* safe here," Umosogo whispered hoarsely. "Umosogo, he go and the bad men follow him. But they not catch him—Umosogo too clever."

"But how shall I get out of here?" gasped Peter.

"Umosogo, he come at dawn for the *Nkosana*. Fear not, but do not stir; it is not good to wander in the *bundu*."

For an instant Umosogo's face hovered over his young master, then it was gone. The cries of the chase were terrifyingly close. Before them, Umosogo ran as lightly and swiftly as a gazelle. Within a few minutes the poachers burst through the bushes beside the place where Peter lay hidden. Peter held his breath and crouched even lower. His heart beat so loudly that it seemed to him they must hear it.

Uncertain which way to turn, the men paused. Peter could hear their heavy breathing. He felt them turn toward the place where he lay hidden. Surely now they must find him! He braced himself and summoned his courage. Then a low whistle sounded, a voice called savagely, "This way," and they were gone. Peter listened as they sped off into the bush. For the moment he was safe, but how could Umosogo escape so remorseless a pack?

The sounds of the chase faded away, and Peter was left alone. There was nothing for him to do but wait for dawn. He put his hand in his pocket, and his fingers touched something hard. He pulled out the pearl and fingered it gently. A moonbeam penetrated the thick darkness, and he held the stone in the pale shaft of light. He turned it this way and that, letting the light flash and glimmer on its flawless surface. Thoughtfully he replaced it in his pocket.

Out of the darkness came the eerie, chuckling call of the hyena. Its high screaming laughter echoed and re-echoed through the bushveldt.

Shivering violently, Peter put his hands over his ears in a vain attempt to shut out the sound. It was, he thought wildly, as if all the evil spirits of the bush—about which Umosogo had so often warned him—were laughing at his plight. The ghostly sounds faded and the night was still. Only the wind sighed gently in the branches and the endless throbbing song of the cicadas beat out the passing seconds. To Peter the pulsing song seemed to beat out the rhythm of Umosogo's hunted feet. Beads of sweat gathered coldly on Peter's forehead. Suppose Umosogo were captured. Who then would come to rescue him? Only Umosogo knew where he was. Suppose Umosogo, even if he did escape, could not find the place. Suppose no one ever found him? A host of fearful thoughts passed through Peter's mind.

Somewhere, a long way off, a lion roared. Peter sat up and listened intently. He desperately wished that he had a gun; his small knife was little protection. He began to feel cold and damp. He thought of his home and his parents. What were they doing now? He wondered how long it was till dawn.

Umosogo ran on. At first he was confident that he would soon shake off his pursuers. But it was not long before he realized that he must exert himself to the utmost if he were to escape them. The sounds of the chase still echoed behind him. With an effort he increased his pace. His long legs strode swiftly over the hard ground. Often he stopped to listen, then he would turn suddenly and run at right angles to his former track.

The miles passed. Umosogo slowed his gliding run to a brisk walk. Now, when he stopped to listen, he could hear nothing. He grinned with satisfaction. Had not Umosogo, as cunning as the hare, outwitted his enemies?

Now that the immediate danger was over, Umosogo

realized how tired and hungry he was. He could not remember when he had last eaten. He walked on a little, looking about him for some jikijola berries. To his surprise, only a few hundred yards to his right he saw the faint flicker of flames. Eagerly he started toward them. He burst through a thin screen of trees and saw a fire burning merrily in the center of a small clearing. Huddled over it, his back to Umosogo, was a lone figure.

Cautiously Umosogo edged around the fire until he was looking toward the face of the man who crouched there over a simmering pot of porridge. It was Old Jabula!

"*Sakubona,* Jabula," said Umosogo.

"*Sakubona,* Umosogo," replied the old man calmly.

Umosogo sank wearily down by the fire, his eyes still on the old man's face.

"What does Jabula here? Why has he left his master?"

"The time has come. It is not good for Jabula to stay with *Inkosi* any more."

Umosogo did not understand, for his senses were half numbed with hunger and exhaustion. He put out his hand. "I am very hungry," he said simply.

For answer, the old man reached for the porridge pot. Carefully he took it from the fire. He poured a quantity of its contents into a rough wooden bowl, which he held out to his visitor.

Umosogo took the food eagerly. Dimly he wondered why Jabula had shown no surprise at their sudden meeting; why he had not asked how it happened that Umosogo was wandering in the bush so far from home.

Jabula offered his visitor a gourd brimming over with millet beer. Umosogo grasped the gourd and drained the beer to the last drop. He smiled at Old Jabula and started to rise, but he could not; his legs would not hold him. Again he tried and half-staggered to his feet; again he fell back. Bewildered, he lay still.

As if from a long way off, Jabula's voice came to him, very low and gentle. "Sleep, my son, sleep. But a little time only, and all will be well."

Bravely Umosogo struggled against the great tiredness that swept over him. Suddenly he had no more strength; exhausted, he lay back. Old Jabula was right; he must sleep—but only for a few moments. Then he must return to *Nkosana*.

Before his wavering gaze the dancing flames in the fire advanced and retreated. Suddenly the whole world seemed filled with flickering redness. Umosogo struggled to raise his head, but he could not. He had a dim impression of someone bending over him. He felt the cool touch of a finger on his leaden eyelids. Then sleep came, and he remembered nothing more.

Old Jabula straightened up, a small smile of triumph on his face. He picked up the empty gourd. The drug had done its work. Umosogo would sleep now for many hours. Nothing could wake him.

LOST

*D*AWN came at last, then sunrise. Impatiently now Peter waited for Umosogo, but there was no sign of him. The minutes seemed like hours. He watched with interest a widow bird, heavy with dew, drying its feathers in the first rays of the sun. After a while the bird flew away with a curious rising and falling motion.

Stiffly Peter climbed out of his hiding place and stood up, uncertain what to do. He looked all around. The bush stretched out with a terrifying sameness. In the far distance he could just make out the dim outline of a flat-topped hill, taller than those around it. He would head for that high hill, he decided. From there he could see the country laid out like a map.

Beside him there was a sudden rustle in the long grass. Peter stood frozen to the spot. When he saw nothing, he told himself it must have been a snake or a bird.

It was now broad daylight, and still there was no sign of Umosogo. For a little longer Peter lingered. Then, quite suddenly and without a backward glance, he set off in the direction of the high hill.

On and on Peter walked. The hill was farther away than he had thought.

He was very thirsty, and he could not remember when he had last eaten. He came at last on a bush of jikijola berries, only a few, but better than nothing.

It was very hot, but he struggled on. Often the grass and the thorn trees were so high that they shut out his view. Once he glimpsed the distant hill, but it seemed hardly nearer than when he had started. Peter did not know how long he had been walking, but he judged that it was afternoon, as already the sun was sinking toward the west.

He came to a clearing. A herd of zebra and wildebeest, startled from their afternoon siesta, galloped off in a cloud of dust. The black-and-white striped flanks of the zebra were bright against the dull hides of the wildebeest. To Peter's eyes the zebra seemed poorly camouflaged in the strong light.

He startled a giraffe nibbling the young leaves of a mimosa tree. It regarded Peter for a moment out of huge, long-lashed eyes, then ambled gracefully off. As Peter continued to watch, the giraffe broke into a curious rocking-horse canter. Although seemingly un-

hurried, it disappeared from view with remarkable speed. At last only the slender, purple-and-tawny-patched neck showed above the scrub, looking, Peter thought, like some weird creature from a prehistoric age.

He found another jikijola bush and gladly picked its berries. As he stood slowly chewing the last of them, a flash of brilliant color caught his eye. Frowning, he walked on a few paces. For a moment he forgot his distress at the sight which met his eyes.

Sunk in the red earth was a tiny pool, bright and blue as the sky above, and fringed with a fantastic mosaic of brilliant butterflies. Eagerly Peter ran to the pool. The butterflies rose in a kaleidoscopic whirl of emerald, crimson, saffron, and violet, their soft wings brushing his face. Unheeding, he flung himself down and, thrusting his burning face into the cool water, drank until he could drink no more. The water was fresh and sweet, it ran coldly down his parched throat.

Peter sat down beneath the spreading branches of a tree. I'll rest here a little, he thought, and laid his head on the greenish-gray moss. In a few moments he had drifted off into the deep sleep of exhaustion. The bush starlings hopped about the sleeping figure. A troop of monkeys rustled in a nearby tree and chattered among themselves, then swung gaily away.

The shadows were long on the ground before Peter awoke. At first he could not remember where he was. Sleepily he rubbed his eyes, then sat up. Sunset! The terrible realization dawned. He was alone in the *bundu* with the night approaching. He jumped to his feet, almost crying in his despair. Why had he allowed himself to sleep? The whole day was gone; already the daylight was fading. Soon he would be unable to see his way. He shuddered as he thought of night in the bush, with the wild beasts all around.

Hurriedly he set off again in the direction of the hill. He saw it dark and large in the distance. On and on he went, trying not to think of the stories he had read and heard of travelers lost in the bush. Yet he could not help remembering how they wandered in endless circles until they died from exhaustion, despair, and hunger. And how some who did survive lived on in a madness caused by thirst and the heat of the sun.

He stopped to call for help, but no one answered, and the sound of his voice echoed mockingly on the clear evening air. Again and again he shouted, but all was silent. A monkey chattered, its voice sounding strangely human. A green parrot looked at him curiously as he passed.

Kites wheeled in the evening sky from which the glow had faded. Soon darkness fell on the bushveldt, and the night noises began. All around him Peter heard faint rustling and moving sounds. He broke into a run, then steadied, and forced himself to walk on calmly.

He must find a tree, he decided, where he could spend the night in comparative safety. But where to find such a tree? The thorn trees, which he could just see in the pale moonlight, were too low. Besides, their thorns made them impossible to climb. The other trees had no branches low enough for him to grip. The trunks of the blue gum trees were so smooth, straight, and slender that there was scarcely a foothold for a monkey.

In despair Peter tried to fight down his rising panic. Why had he ever left his hiding place? Perhaps even in the cave of the pearls he had been better off!

Quite near him a leopard snarled viciously, the sound vibrating in the night air. Terror gripped Peter, and he broke into a run. He did not know where he was going, only that somehow he must escape from this place. As he ran, the very branches of the trees seemed to reach out to hold him back. Their black shadows shifted eerily on the ground. Again the snarl sounded, nearer this time. On and on plunged Peter, forcing himself to run even faster.

Without warning, his strength failed and he fell headlong on the hard, dry ground. He lay stunned for a time, then opened his eyes and wearily raised his head.

There, only a few feet away, stood the Golden Impala, the first of all the impala, the guardian of its kind. Peter again looked into the amber eyes of *Okhanyayo,* the Shining One of the legend. In them he saw mirrored the dappled pools, the green shadows, the hot bright sunlight on the yellow plains. For a brief instant he glimpsed the undiscovered past and the vanishing future of the whole impala race.

Cautiously Peter rose to his feet and stretched out his hand. The Impala did not move, except to turn its graceful head. Peter saw that the ridges on its arched horns flashed and sparkled.

Peter took a step toward the Shining One. The animal bounded out of reach but remained in sight, watching the boy. Again Peter stepped forward. Again the animal retreated.

The Impala stood beneath a large wild fig tree with low, wide-spreading branches. Only a few paces separated it from Peter. Suddenly a distant thudding startled the Impala. It jerked away and disappeared. Peter ran after it a little way, but no familiar gleam shone in the darkness.

The crashing noise sounded again, much nearer this time. Peter darted back and climbed as quickly as he could into the safety of the fig tree. A startled polecat snarled, its eyes shining pin-point green, then darted away.

It was an easy climb, but Peter did not rest until he was high off the ground, securely wedged between two thick, twisted branches. As he peered down, a buffalo stamped into the clearing. It lowered its wicked head, its horns hooked menacingly. Peter held his breath. He had heard terrible tales of buffalo circling a tree for days, until its victim fell to the ground overcome with hunger and exhaustion. But this buffalo sniffed the air, glanced around, and moved away.

Peter prepared to settle for the night. He managed to wedge his body securely between the intertwining branches, so that he would not fall. Through the leaves the stars glittered like diamonds. The night wind sighed. Lightly the leaves seemed to whisper: "Four

times shall you see him—once, twice, thrice; but the fourth time beware."

So it had come. The third time was past. There remained only the fourth and last time.

LEROUX

W HEN Leroux and his gang leaped ashore in pursuit of Umosogo and Peter, Leroux had little doubt that they would soon catch them. For what match were a boy and a native for Leroux and his armed gang?

They made good progress through the bush in the bright moonlight. Leroux expected to come on their prey at any moment. But they did not. They burst into a small clearing and paused beside a much-overgrown bush, panting heavily and wondering which direction to take.

Then one of the Shangaans whistled shrilly and set off at great speed along the narrow game track. Leroux followed unquestioningly, for he knew the ability of native trackers. They were reputed to be able to hear at night things that a white man would miss even by day.

The moments passed, but still there was no sign of the two. Leroux felt a surge of fury. How dare they escape him—Leroux the bold, Leroux the cunning?

Ahead, the Shangaan tracker halted and murmured uncertainly to his companion. Furious at the delay, Leroux yelled, "What are you stopping for? Get on, men. Get on, I say."

The two natives turned to their master with wildly staring eyes. They began to speak in their halting English.

"Get on, get on, you useless dogs," Leroux broke in savagely. And to give point to his words he raised his rifle.

Frightened, the Shangaans whispered to each other in their own language, then set off once more into the bush. They traveled so fast that the others found it very hard to keep up with them. Except Leroux, who ran like a man possessed. Each time the Shangaans stopped he drove them on with brutal words and threats.

Leroux and his gang had been running for a long time. One by one the stars faded. Soon it would be dawn. How many miles they had come they did not know. They had traveled so fast that they had scarcely noticed the passing of the hours. Several times members of the gang implored their leader to stop, but he would not. Pointing to the lightening sky, he declared, "We'll see them when it's daylight."

The sun rose, and they felt its warm rays on their faces. Higher and higher it climbed, until it beat down hotly upon them.

Without warning the Shangaans stopped dead. They turned to Leroux. "Go no more, *Inkosi*. No find."

"What do you mean?" yelled Leroux.

The Shangaans gazed at him with wide, terrified eyes and did not answer. Something in their expression made Max step forward. He addressed them in their own language, quietly and without anger. Eagerly they turned to him and poured out a long tale. The rest of the party, unable to understand, studied Max's face. They saw an expression of dismay spread over his dark features, followed by a grim, almost sneering smile.

The Shangaans ended their tale. Max folded his arms and turned to Leroux, his face expressionless.

"Well?" asked Leroux. "Out with it."

"They say that there are no more tracks. They say that they lost tracks soon after that last stop in the clearing. They say that they were so terrified by your shouts and threats that they pretended to see tracks where there were none. Now they are tired and will go no farther."

With something like a snarl Leroux started toward the two Shangaans. But Max laid a warning hand on his arm and spoke very low. "You have done enough harm already," he told Leroux. "If you drive them too far they will leave us, and we will all die here. We need their help to guide us out of the bush. Dispose of them afterward if you must, but not now. I suggest that we let them guide us back, the way we came, and give up the idea of catching those two for the present."

Reluctantly Leroux agreed. They decided to rest during the heat of the day, then to get as far as they could on the return journey before night fell.

They came upon a large wild fig tree, and settled down beneath its spreading branches. Protected from the worst glare of the sun and too exhausted to search for food or water, they drifted off into an uneasy sleep.

It was nearly evening before they stood up stiffly and moved along on the return journey. For a while they strode in silence, the two Shangaans leading the way. A solitary polecat darted across their path. Instantly their guides stopped.

"What is it now?" growled Leroux.

Once again Max stepped forward. As before, he listened to the natives without comment. Then he answered them gently, pointing to his gun. They seemed reassured, but as they walked on they glanced warily from side to side.

Max dropped back to Leroux's side. "They say it's unlucky to see a polecat," Max told Leroux. "They were babbling about devils and spirits. I told them that we would protect them with white man's magic and gave them a lot of talk about the power of the guns. But they're still pretty jumpy. I can't quite understand it."

Leroux frowned and shrugged. "Well done, Max," he admitted. "What we all need now is some food and drink. I suggest that we fan out a little. You and I, Max, will stay with these fellows—" he indicated the Shangaans— "and the others can try to shoot some game."

Most of the gang disappeared a few yards into the

bush. Max saw a large speckled guinea fowl on the path ahead and, as it fluttered toward the long grass, he raised his gun and fired.

From the grass came a loud yell of pain and fury. The guinea fowl flapped away screeching but unharmed, but Karl staggered onto the track groaning noisily. Max's shot had entered the fleshy part of his shoulder. He was more frightened than hurt. The wound, though undoubtedly painful, was not serious.

Leroux gazed at Karl with contempt. Max knelt down to bind the injury with a large, red-spotted handkerchief, while Leroux fingered his red beard, and the two Shangaans stared at the wounded man. As Max helped Karl, still moaning and grumbling, to his feet, he caught the look of terror on the natives' faces.

"What's the matter with you two?" Max asked them.

"The Spirit of the Bush is angry," they told him. "He seeks revenge for the impala. First the polecat ran across our path; now the white *Inkosi* is shot."

Max could see that their faith in the power of the white man's magic was shaken because of the accident, while their faith in the Spirit of the Bush was stronger.

The morale of the party had fallen very low. Even Jake's return with a small buck he had shot did not raise it much.

As night was approaching, they made a rough camp. They roasted the meat over a fire and ate Kaffir oranges off a nearby tree. But they could not shake their uneasy feeling. Unconsciously they edged near the fire and never loosened their hold on their guns. As the night

closed in they spoke only in low whispers. Around them
mosquitoes hovered and the myriad small noises of the
bush sounded in their ears. They lay down by the fire,
but sleep did not come.

Just before dawn an owl hooted once. Instantly the
two Shangaans sprang to their feet. "*Isikhova! Isikhova!*" they shrieked. Only the threat of the guns pre-
vented them from rushing headlong into the night.

"The owl," echoed Steiger, his face pale.

"What is all this?" asked Leroux furiously.

"I have heard that it is not good to hear an owl hoot
once in the night," Steiger told his leader. "It means
that someone is going to die. One of us, Leroux. It must
be one of us."

There was a long silence. The natives, too terrified to
move, cowered near the fire, their faces buried in their
hands. They rocked themselves to and fro on their heels,
and repeated over and over the single word "*Okhanyayo.*"

Max leaned forward, his face very serious. "I don't
like this," he said to Leroux.

"Ask them what they mean," Leroux insisted.

But to Max's questions they steadily refused to reply.
Max shook his head. "Whatever it is, Leroux, they will
never tell us."

"I'll see about that," cried Leroux. He sprang to his
feet and bent over the two natives. "Speak," he hissed.
"Speak."

Terrified, they shrank back.

"Speak," Leroux said again, "or else, by heaven, I

will shoot you both." He shouldered his rifle and aimed straight at one of them. When he raised his finger to the trigger, the already unnerved Shangaans had had enough. Their control snapped, and together they shrieked wildly into the night.

"Beware the Shining One!" they shouted in their native tongue. "Beware the Shining One."

Leroux lowered his gun. "What do you mean? Answer me."

In a low halting voice, punctuated with much rolling of the eyes and violent shivering, one of them began to tell the strange legend. Max translated it into English, sentence by sentence. The native told them of the Golden Impala and its mission to save its race from destruction, and of the white boy, *Okhethiwe.*

The group around the fire listened intently. A fine drifting mist swirled through the bush. It shrouded the huddled thorn trees, shutting out the sky until there was only the flickering fire and the voice that spoke of things they did not understand, of things beyond the reach of guns and violence.

Suddenly, as the story came to an end, they were afraid. All save Leroux.

For a moment no one spoke. Then Leroux threw back his head and laughed. The harsh, sneering laughter echoed and re-echoed through the bush.

"What a pack of lies! Who ever heard of a Golden Impala? None of you has ever seen one and none of you ever will. All that nonsense about this *Okhethiwe!* I'm

not afraid of spirits or whatever you want to call them.
Let them do their worst. I'm ready for them."

Ashamed of their fears, the other white men watched
their leader with grudging admiration. Of course he
was right, they told themselves. The whole thing was
mere superstition.

Smiling scornfully, Leroux sprang to his feet and
walked a little beyond the firelit circle. There he stood
for a moment, gazing into the thinning mist and carelessly swinging his gun. He spoke half to himself but,
although they could not see his face, the muttered words
carried distinctly on the still air.

"If I ever see this Golden Impala I'll shoot it. Do you
hear? Shoot it, shoot it!" He broke into a low, chuckling
laugh.

His companions stared at one another uneasily. Abruptly the mirthless laughter was cut short. For as Leroux swung around to face them, Max saw that their
leader's face was deathly pale and that his eyes glittered
oddly.

"Did you see it?" Leroux's voice sounded high, un-
natural. "It was there, I tell you, standing quite still in
the mist. It was watching us, shining—" He broke off and
swung away from them.

"There it is again. After it, all of you!"

Leroux's voice rose to a scream, and he plunged headlong into the bush. For an instant the others hesitated
as they struggled with a sickening fear.

"Come on!" Leroux's voice was fainter.

The next moment the men were running through

the bush after Leroux. As they ran their confidence returned. They would follow this man who was not afraid of shadows. Leroux would prove that he was stronger and braver than any man alive, stronger than superstition, stronger than the dread Spirit of the Bush.

THE FOURTH TIME

*P*ETER was warned of the approach of dawn by the distant booming of a hornbill. He was feeling stiff and sore but much less tired after his few hours' sleep. He took a careful look around, then swung down from his hiding place. For breakfast he found and ate some water berries.

Peter could not see the hill, but he set off in the direction where he judged it lay. Surely today he must reach it!

Three sable antelope in single file stepped onto the path ahead of him. In the weak light their dark chestnut coats looked almost black, the white cheeks showed palely. Their long, sharp, back-sweeping horns made Peter's heart hammer uncomfortably. But the antelope,

137

sighting the intruder, bounded away so swiftly that
Peter could barely follow them with his eye.

With the coming of the light, new hope surged up in
Peter. He walked briskly. He did not see any more game
—only an emerald snake that slid away into the grass in
front of him. The going was easy, for he was following
a game track. The bush was a network of these tracks,
to and from the water holes, places of shelter, and good
grazing grounds. Peter tried not to think about lion or
leopard, but as he walked he glanced nervously from
side to side.

The sun rose higher, and Peter's confidence began
to dwindle. There seemed to be something familiar
about the place, and he began to wonder if he were
going mad, like the travelers in the stories. The feeling
of familiarity persisted. He walked on a few steps,
stopped, then retraced his steps. As he looked around,
puzzled, he saw something which made his heart pound.
There, only a few feet from where he stood, was the
over-grown bush beneath which Umosogo had hidden
him. He had come in a full circle. Peter gave a cry of
despair which echoed mournfully through the bush.

It was then that he had an idea so startlingly simple
that he was amazed he had not thought of it before.
Somewhere, not too far from here, was the river. If he
could reach it, he could follow it down until he reached
some form of civilization. Or, if he dared, he could head
upstream, past the cave and the fatal clearing, and from
there on home. It seemed an eternity since he had seen
his home.

He felt elated with his idea. He had only to find the river, then everything would be all right. With renewed hope Peter left the hiding place and tried to go in the direction from which he and Umosogo had come.

The distant boom of a bittern made Peter know that he was near water. Nothing, he told himself, nothing must go wrong now. He looked around him but he could see no one. Cautiously he moved forward, stepping lightly and pausing every few minutes to listen, in case some member of the gang still lurked there to trap him.

Ahead, the ground rose steeply. On the crest of a hill, tall grasses were silhouetted against the sky, their feathery tops bent gracefully in the slight breeze. Peter hurried to the top, parted the grass, and looked down. Immediately below grew a small, stunted tree beside a dark, shining pool. Mirrored in the pool's cool surface was the head of the Golden Impala.

This, then, was the fourth time! Expectantly, Peter waited, but nothing happened. He felt a surge of disappointment. Was the legend not true? Was he not *Okhethiwe,* the Chosen? What of Old Jabula's warning?

The Impala raised its head from the water and saw Peter. It leaped over the pool, a little distance to the right of him. There it stopped and began to nibble some tender shoots. Peter climbed carefully down the bank and skirted the pool behind the stunted tree. He slid into the long grass only a few yards from the Impala.

A slight sound made him glance back over his shoulder toward the bank. There, huge on the skyline, he saw Leroux, his rifle aimed directly at the Impala, ready to shoot.

Without a thought, Peter leaped from the grass and hurled himself in front of the Impala. There was a deafening sound. Shocked, Peter shut his eyes. When he looked again, the Impala was out of range, but still in view. Leroux, startled by the suddenness of Peter's appearance, had missed.

Peter turned to face his enemy; bravely he stared into the barrel of the gun. He saw Max leap up the bank and wrench the gun downward. "You fool!" he heard Max shout.

Scarcely sensing what he saw and heard, Peter watched Jake, Karl, and Steiger run breathlessly to their leader.

"The Shangaans have gone!" they told him. "They heard a shot and made off into the bush. What are we to do?"

Leroux acted as if he did not understand. He laughed wildly, then stopped abruptly. Eyes fixed on the Impala, gun in hand, he sprang down the bank. As he passed, Peter glimpsed the evil, gloating expression on Leroux's face and shrank back in dread.

For an instant the group on the bank hesitated, then they ran down it and, almost without stopping, Jake seized Peter and flung him roughly onto his shoulder. Off they went, running between the thorn trees and through the long grass, leaping great cracks in the red earth, on and on without a pause. Jake, half carrying, half dragging Peter, tried to keep up with the others.

All the time the Impala remained in view but always just out of range.

Directly ahead loomed a flat-topped hill. On one side of it a steep rock cliff formed a narrow ravine. Without hesitation the Impala leaped up onto the flat slabs of rock. As the pursuers reached the first boulders the Impala began to climb. It leaped gracefully from rock to rock, up and up the steep cliff.

Awestruck, they all stood watching. Halfway up the Impala paused. Leroux aimed and pulled the trigger. Nothing happened. The magazine of the gun was empty. Unharmed, the Shining One climbed on.

Maddened, Leroux swung around and tore Karl's gun from his hands. He fired and fired again, until that gun, too, was empty. But the shots only echoed and re-echoed down the rocks of the ravine.

With a final bound the Impala gained the topmost rock and looked down. Silhouetted black against the sun, high above the watchers, it lowered its sweeping horns menacingly. A cold wind blew down the ravine and the men shivered.

Unhurriedly the Impala stepped lightly onto the far edge of the rock. It stamped its forefeet once, then leaped down, and they saw it no more.

"Through the ravine!" cried Leroux. "We'll cut it off as it comes down the other side."

"No more ammunition," yelled Jake.

But Leroux paid no heed. Stumbling over the boulders, he ran into the mouth of the ravine. They were in the pass now, in single file. Leroux ran in front, the rest straggled behind him, Peter still roughly gripped by Jake's strong left hand.

Above the sound of their own thudding feet, Peter became aware of a dull throbbing sound ahead of them. Every second it grew louder. In the distance he could see approaching something that looked like a great brown wave. As it came nearer, Peter realized that it was a surging mass of impala packed in the ravine.

Horrified, the men halted. The red dust was being whirled into the air by countless thousands of sharp, drumming hoofs. Panic-stricken, the gang raced for the shelter of the rocks and desperately climbed the steep face of the cliff. Jake had dropped Peter's hand to free himself for the climb. Somehow Peter scrambled to safety on an overhanging ledge, where he clung for his life.

Only Leroux still stood in the path of the approaching stampede. Deaf to all warning shouts he continued to stand there, vainly brandishing his useless gun.

Surely, thought Peter, he cannot think that he, alone, can turn the impala? He gazed at Leroux with reluctant admiration, fascinated in spite of himself. The stampede was very close now, and still the red-bearded man stood in the path of the flailing hoofs. They were almost on him.

Suddenly his nerve snapped. With a scream of terror, Leroux hurled his empty weapon at the foremost impala and threw himself at the steep side of the rock. Frantically his fingers clawed for a hand-hold. He heaved himself up just as the great herd thundered beneath him, a

whirling, surging confusion of horns and wildly staring eyes. Then, without warning, the rock to which he clung gave way, and he plunged downward. For an instant he was borne along on the heaving backs, then was swallowed up in the turbulent sea of bodies.

SEVENTEEN

SIGN IN THE DUST

*W*HEN Umosogo awoke from his drugged sleep, the clearing was deserted. All that remained of the fire were a few ashes. He sat up, wearily rubbing his heavy eyes. His whole body ached, and there was a throbbing pain in his head.

Umosogo looked around, bewildered. What was he doing here? He glanced down and saw the empty porridge bowl at his side. In a flash he remembered. He had found Old Jabula, and Jabula had given him food and drink. Then he had fallen asleep.

Aghast, Umosogo saw by the sun that it was late afternoon. He had slept through the whole day!

Frantically he struggled to his feet and stood swaying unsteadily. Only with a supreme effort of will could he manage to remain upright. He knew now what had happened—Old Jabula had drugged him; there had been something in the gourd of beer, and the drug had done its work well.

Wearily, he passed his hand over his forehead. *Nkosana* had waited in vain. Umosogo had failed his young master. Where was *Nkosana* now?

Blindly the tall dark man started forward. As he hurried back in the direction he had come, his mind grew clearer. He began to think of the legend of the Shining One. He remembered that the Chosen One must go alone or all would be lost.

Alone. His young master was alone. The realization bit deep into Umosogo's consciousness. He broke into a stumbling run—then stopped. He was torn between his fear of offending the Spirit of the Bush and his great loyalty to the Ward family. The thought that Old Jabula had been sent by the Spirit to stop him from returning to *Nkosana* was a frightening thought. But Umosogo was a brave man and a loyal one. Thrusting aside his fears, he pressed on.

It was nearly dark when he reached the empty hiding place. There he saw what he so much feared—the hiding place was empty. *Nkosana* was gone.

Anxiously he searched the ground for some trace of the missing boy. Half hidden in the grass at his feet he saw a small shining object. He stooped and picked it up. It was a white jewel of a rare size and beautiful texture. Puzzled, Umosogo turned it over in the palm of his hand, but it told him nothing. The one thing for him to do, he decided, was to return to Thabankwe and get help as quickly as possible. Else none of them might ever again see *Nkosana*.

It was very early in the morning when Umosogo staggered through the garden to the warden's house. As he reached the steps a game ranger started down them. Before the man could speak, Umosogo cried, "Take me to *Inkosi!*"

The next instant he was in the room with the distracted Wards, Richard Hutchison, and Philip Keen. They were consulting with the rangers for yet another and wider search for Peter.

"*Inkosi!*"

Hector Ward whirled around. "Umosogo! Where is *Nkosana?*"

Umosogo saw that his master's face was drawn and his eyes red from lack of sleep. Quickly he told his story. As they listened, everyone in the room sat very still, shaken by the tale. Umosogo's voice trailed off.

"Peter is alone, Hector! Alone in that awful bush. How are we ever to find him?" Mrs. Ward's voice rose hysterically. Mr. Ward gently put an arm around his wife's shoulders.

"*Inkosi! Inkosi!*" someone called loudy from outside. It was John, the native cook, rounding the corner of the house. As he came into the house he caught sight of Umosogo, stopped dead, and broke into an excited torrent in his own language.

"What is it, Umosogo? What has happened?" Mr. Ward interrupted. "Is there any news of Peter?"

Umosogo shook his head. "No, *Inkosi*. Old Jabula
. . ."

"But Jabula disappeared two days ago!"

"Yes, *Inkosi*. But this morning John go to Old Jabula's kraal to see if he come back. He not find Jabula
but he say there is a sign."

"A sign? What does it mean?"

"Umosogo not know, but *Inkosi* and Umosogo must
go and see." Unconsciously he spoke with authority.

When Hector Ward and Umosogo reached Jabula's
kraal, they looked down together at a few faint scratches
freshly made in the dust.

"I don't think this means anything," said Mr. Ward.
Disappointed, he turned to go.

"Wait, *Inkosi*." Umosogo knelt and traced the
scratches with his finger. Then he jumped up and went
to the other side of the drawing. From there he looked
long and hard at it. He gave a great shout.

"The hill, *Inkosi!* See, there is the flat rock!" He
jabbed excitedly at the drawing with his foot. "There,
the great cliffs."

Mr. Ward looked again and saw that Umosogo was
indeed right. In the dust was a crude but recognizable
map of the hill, well known in the area for its distinctive
flat top. It could be no other place.

"It is a sign, *Inkosi*. We must go there." Umosogo
was almost overcome with excitement.

Still Mr. Ward hesitated. "Will we find *Nkosana*
there?" he asked.

"Who can say?" replied Umosogo sadly. "But Jabula

has spoken. He has given us a sign, and we must obey."

"We have nothing else to go on," said Mr. Ward. "All right. We'll go."

In a short time Mr. Ward, Philip, Richard, Umosogo, and the rangers drove off on their way to the flat-topped hill.

THE MARK

T HEY went as far as possible toward their objective by car. Then, some four or five miles from the hill, they left the two cars and set off on foot.

When they were within a mile or so of the hill, they were startled by a burst of firing.

"Come on!" yelled Mr. Ward. "After those devils!"

Gaining the bottom of the hill, Hector ordered the rangers and Philip to the right. He, Richard, and Umosogo took the left. Above them they heard the frantic shrieks of the baboons. They saw the stampede of impala sweep from the mouth of the ravine out onto the plain. Jostling through the last of the straggling animals, Hector ran on, half blinded and choked by the thick dust. Glancing up, he saw a small figure huddled on a ledge.

"Peter!" Hector Ward gasped hoarsely. "Thank heaven!"

Peter tried to speak but no words came. Richard and Umosogo ran up.

"Is he all right?" asked Richard anxiously.

"I think so," said Mr. Ward, a smile on his dust-stained face.

"The poachers," gasped Peter. "That way." With an effort he pointed up the far end of the ravine.

"Don't worry, Pete. Our men at the other end will get them."

Peter gave a great sigh of relief and lost consciousness.

Umosogo lifted the boy in his arms. "It is well, *Nkosana,*" he said.

When Peter woke up later that afternoon he was lying in a hammock on the stoop of his home. His mother smiled down at him. "Hello, darling," she said, and bent to hug him. Sleepily he glanced around. His father and Richard sat close by.

"Where's Philip?" Peter asked.

"He went off. Didn't say where. Said he'd be back tonight," replied Mr. Ward.

Peter pulled himself into a sitting position. "What's happened?" he asked, puzzled. "How did I get here? What became of Umosogo?"

Mr. Ward told his son of Umosogo's return, of Old Jabula's appearance and message, of their journey to the hill, and of how they had found him there. He added that the rangers had captured Max and the rest of the gang.

"Not Leroux," Peter said quietly. "Leroux is dead."

Mrs. Ward spoke suddenly. "We've been nearly frantic with worry, darling. Tell us what happened to you, if you feel strong enough."

Fascinated, they listened as Peter told his strange story. When he finished, for a moment no one spoke.

"So the legend of the Golden Impala was true after all," said Mr. Ward thoughtfully. "The impala were seeking the safety of the reserves. But even there they were not safe. Your part in it was to protect the Golden Impala from the killer. And that you did at the risk of your own life." Mr. Ward's voice broke. He glanced down at his watch on his wrist. "The police will be here soon," he said in a more natural tone of voice.

"Police!" exclaimed Peter. "Why?"

"Because there are two Shangaans not yet accounted for. Umosogo told us about the cave, and we think they might have gone there. From what you have told us, it looks as though we were right to send Professor Hardy to the cave with them. He has come down here from Johannesburg—on a clue to trace the theft of his papers."

"I hope they find the pearls," Peter said. "They are gorgeous. But I hope no one will ever make another one."

Hector Ward and Richard Hutchison thought of the dreadful scene of the slaughtered impala and silently nodded their heads.

Just then a large car drew up in front of the house. A police inspector accompanied a harassed-looking short man up the steps. "Everyone accounted for, sir."

"Well done, indeed," said Mr. Ward.

The inspector went on, "We captured the two Shangaans, sir." He noticed Peter in the hammock and said, "I'd like to talk to the boy here, but perhaps I'd better come back tomorrow for that. I'll wait for you in the car, Professor."

The little man laid a black box on the table and took a chair.

Peter looked for a second at the black box, then sprang out of the hammock. "The pearls!" he cried, and, without asking the professor's permission, he flung back the lid. Then, with an exclamation of horrified surprise he slammed down the lid so violently that the box fell from the table onto the floor. A heap of bright, white powder spilled out. Aghast and bewildered, Peter knelt down and ran his fingers through the dust.

The professor smiled ruefully. "As you see," he said, "my experiment was only a temporary success. I had hoped for something better. But after the papers with my formula were stolen I did more work, and I did suspect that any success might not be lasting. Those gentlemen were in too great a hurry to believe what they wanted to believe."

"But I don't understand," said Peter. "Where are the pearls?"

"I discovered," the professor went on, "that in these pearls there must be an infinitesimal trace of water to hold the tiny molecules in stability. This, the secretion supplies. But no scientist can make the exact compensation for constant changes in the atmosphere. When the delicate water balance is disturbed, the pearls collapse into dust—as you see."

"Can the experiment ever succeed?" asked Mr. Ward anxiously.

"I fear not." The professor sighed. "No, I'm afraid that the secretion has no more than a biological interest." He turned to look at Peter. "No one will wish to harm the impala now," he said. "Now I must go. Good-by, Peter. And thank you for helping me to get my papers back."

He held out his hand to Mrs. Ward and then to Mr. Ward. "Please thank Umosogo for taking me to the cave," he said as he picked up the box.

"You know," said Mr. Ward thoughtfully as he shook hands with the professor, "we owe a tremendous debt to Umosogo. More than we can ever repay. We must see that his great courage and loyalty do not go unrewarded."

That evening, Peter stood at the window of his room. In the empty garden a fine, shifting mist drifted up from the bush.

Footsteps in the hall outside his room made Peter turn. Philip Keen came in and, closing the door softly behind him, leaned against it. His narrow face was stained with red dust.

"Where have you been?" asked Peter.

"Back to the hill."

"Why?" pleaded Peter. "Oh, Philip, there is so much that I don't understand. Why was I chosen? How did the stampede start? Where did the impala go? How could it all have happened?"

Philip smiled and slowly shook his head. "There is a great deal that we will never understand, but three things at least are certain! The impala race is no longer in any danger. *Okhethiwe* saved their leader's life. And *Okhanyayo*—" he paused, and then went on. "*Okhanyayo,* seeing that there was no longer any safety for his kind within the reserves, lured his enemies to destruction."

Peter started violently. "You mean the stampede was called by the Golden Impala?"

"Who can tell," said Philip quietly. "*Okhanyayo* has returned to his kind, and you will not see the Shining One again. The legend, Peter, is almost fulfilled."

"Almost?"

"The legend says that *Okhethiwe* shall know when his task is ended by the mark of the Shining One. On the topmost rock of the hill, at the very edge of the cliff, I found this."

Into Peter's hand Philip thrust a flat, black fragment of rock. On its hard surface was the imprint of an impala's hoof, clearly marked in gold.

Without another word, Philip slipped quietly from the room.

In the dark Peter sat and looked at the piece of rock in his hand. On it faintly gleamed the shining mark— the mark of the Golden Impala.

GLOSSARY

assegai: a kind of hunting spear, used by Zulu and other African tribes.

Basuto: a member of various tribes that live in Basutoland. They are excellent horsemen, and wear colorful blankets and conical straw hats.

biltong: sun-dried strips of salted or spiced meat. Hunters use this as a convenient form of "iron rations."

bundu: native word for bush.

bushveldt: name given to wild South African country. It includes both plains and wooded areas. The words "bush" and "veldt" are also used separately with the same meaning.

grenadilla juice: the juice of the passion flower.

Inkosi: Zulu term of respect. It means "Chief."

isikhova: little owl. This is an object of superstition.

jacaranda tree: a tree common in many parts of Africa,

especially South Africa and Kenya. It has purple
flowers, and is often used for decorative avenues.

jikijola berries: edible berries found in the bush.

Kaffir: Africaans word meaning "native." It is used frequently as an adjective, as "Kaffir dog" to mean a
native dog, or "Kaffir corn" to mean the kind of corn
that is grown in the native villages.

Kaffir boom tree: a large red-flowered tree found in the
bush.

Kaffir oranges: small, bitter fruit found in the bush.

Kikuyu grass: a common variety of tough, coarse, grayish
grass that grows all over Africa.

kraal: a native hut, often made of sun-baked mud or clay.
Kraals are usually thatched with wattle and are
circular in shape.

lesiba: a thin pipe, used by Basuto herd boys. It gives off
a thin, high note.

lumela: a Basuto greeting in common use.

maltabella: a thick brown porridge made of corn. It is a
major food item of African natives.

mealie: corn kernels.

Nkosana: meaning "little chief," it is the word by which
natives address young boys in positions of authority.

ridgeback dog: a cross between a mastiff and a Labrador,
with a long ridge of backward-growing hair on its
back. This stands up even more than normal whenever the dog is angry or alarmed. They are also
sometimes called lion dogs because they used to be
used to hunt lions.

rondavel: an adaptation of the native huts or kraals, built
from a variety of things—mud or clay or wood or
even bricks and mortar—and almost always thatched

with wattle. Rondavels can be large or small, and are frequently used as extra bedrooms for houses.

sakubona: a Zulu greeting, which literally means, "I see you."

Shangaan: a member of a tribe that lives in the northern transvaal.

Swazi: a member of a tribe that lives in Swaziland.

ugubu: a bow-shaped musical instrument with a single string. It is played by rubbing a gourd along the string; this produces variations in tone.

Zulu: a native from Zululand. Zulus are noted for their magnificent physique and fighting qualities. They are fond of wearing animal skins, and Zulu warriors have wonderful head-dresses made of feathers.

DATE DUE			